Hetty

Martha Sears West

Hetty

by

Martha Sears West

CLEAN KIND WORLD
Los Angeles

CLEAN KIND WORLD
Los Angeles
Text and Illustration Copyright © 2014 by Martha Sears West.
Distributed by Ingram Book Company

Library of Congress Cataloging-in-Publication Data
West, Martha Sears, 1938–
Hetty / by Martha Sears West.
pages cm   ISBN 978-0-9886784-7-7
1. Adoption--History--20th century--Fiction.
2. Teenagers--History--20th century--Fiction.
3. Families--History--20th century--Fiction.
4. Parenting--History--20th century- Fiction
5. Psychological fiction.
6. Domestic fiction.
I. Title. PS3623.E449H48 2014   813ʼ.6--dc23
2013048864

www.CleanKindWorldBooks.com   www.ParkPlacePress.com
Toll Free 800·616·8081 · Shipping 435·753·5572 · Fax 323·953·9850
2016 Cummings · Los Angeles CA 90027
ymaddox@CleanKindWorldBooks.com
Martha Sears West titles are available
online and in fine bookstores.
· *Jake, Dad and the Worm* · *Longer Than Forevermore* ·
· *Rhymes and Doodles from a Wind-up Toy* · *Hetty* ·
Hetty is also available in audiobook.

For my parents,
Gordon and Elizabeth Sears,
who provided a home of exceptional love and harmony.

With gratitude to my husband, Steve West,
and for his fifty-three years of support.
Without the inclusion of his experiences in the
Forest Service,
this book would have been
much shorter.

Thanks to
my editor and daughter,
Page Elizabeth West Mallett,
without whose wise advice and insight
I would never have attempted this book
in the first place.

CONTENTS

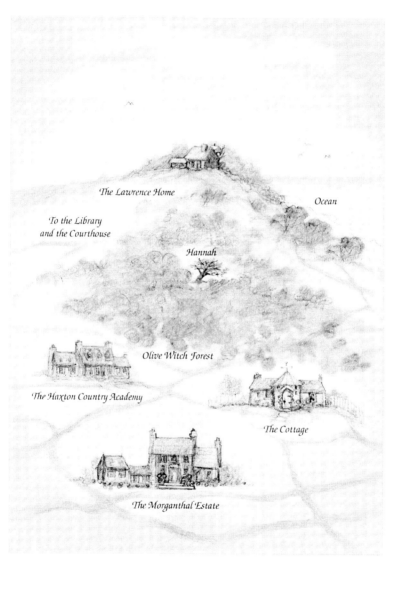

The Lawrence Home

Ocean

To the Library
and the Courthouse

Hannah

Olive Witch Forest

The Haxton Country Academy

The Cottage

The Morganthal Estate

ILLUSTRATIONS

CHARACTERS

Henrietta (*Hetty*) Annette Lawrence

Dan Lawrence (*Papa*)

Dora Lawrence (*Mother*)

Mrs. Freydis Fairburn, *Headmistress of Haxton Academy*

Leaf Locke, *Dan's Forest Service companion*

Anne Locke, *Leaf's wife*

Zack Bond, *firefighter*

Melinda Morganthal, *Hetty's classmate*

Morgan Morganthal, *Melinda's brother*

Marian Reed, *librarian*

CHAPTER ONE

Hetty and Her Hypotenuse Day

Hetty began counting the number of hissing sounds that came through her math teacher's long white teeth with every "s" she pronounced. Her lips were absolutely, positively fire engine-red, and her hair was black as India ink, except for the path that divided her thin strands in the exact mathematical center of her scalp.

When Miss Hacket turned her back to write the day's questions on the blackboard, Hetty decided to attempt a more mathematical appearance herself.

She thought perhaps she would appear better at calculating if the laces of her father's oversized boots looked precisely the same length, so she tucked the two longer ends down into the tops of her socks.

The pencils and books on her desk could use some organizing too. Hetty had discovered the eraser end of a pencil to be the more useful of its two extremes, for math. Therefore, except for the ones she had whittled into totem poles, she zipped the worn ones into her Smokey the Bear pencil case.

Now for the books…would it look better if the blue history book is over or under my French book? It depends on where Miss Hacket's looking from. The red French book should be on top if she's looking down…like if she's on the ceiling or something.

It was easy to picture Miss Hacket's rounded form bouncing aloft against the ceiling panels from where she could peer down at the girls. If she hissed too many s-words, very likely she would gradually deflate, then flop down like a circus tent after the elephants have pulled out the stakes. Hetty hoped Miss Hacket wouldn't use a lot of words like *sassafras* or *Mississippi* if she should happen to be floating directly overhead.

Hetty smoothed the pleats of her plaid uniform and hoped Miss Hacket would notice that she was the most attentive girl in the whole entire sixth grade. She had resolved to keep her eyes absolutely and positively glued to her teacher's lips for the entire fifty-five minutes of class. So Hetty was startled by the squeak of the floorboards as Miss Hacket approached from the left rear. She advanced, wielding a wondrous word.

The word was *Hypotenuse*. Hetty thought it had something to do with triangles or right angles, but it was hissed forth with no accompanying explanation that she could detect. What a grand addition to the day's vocabulary collection! Hetty found such words were infinitely more entertaining when they were allowed to decide their own meaning and usage. She mused on some of the possibilities:

"My, my, what a lovely arrangement of chrysanthemum and hypotenuse blossoms!"

"Waiter, a tall glass of hypotenuse juice, please."

"Take one hypotenuse by mouth, and call me in the morning."

"I apologize for being late for class, Miss Hacket, but you see, my hypotenuse escaped."

"I won't tolerate your constant hypotenusing around, Hetty Annette Lawrence."

"Hetty Annette!" Miss Hacket repeated, "We're on number twelve. Do you know it's your turn?" Hetty wasn't particular about what name people used. She didn't mind being called Hetty or even Netty. It didn't much matter as long as the voice was pleasant.

"Well, I," answered Hetty. "I...um...."

Miss Hacket directed the question to Melinda instead. This gave Hetty a moment to work out a math question of her own: How many minutes would have to pass before the end of the day and time to go home? She had to be content just imagining herself on the way to her house, until at last classes were dismissed in the afternoon.

While approaching her home, Hetty slowly breathed in the soft sea air. She always looked for the small blue patch of ocean that was barely visible through the thick foliage. This time she sang as she walked up the familiar hill, making up a name for each of the tall elm trees that arched over the driveway. It always felt to her as though they had planted themselves there especially to welcome her.

Hetty knew her parents kept her in their thoughts, even though they would still be at work when she got home. Today was no exception. When Hetty reached the sunny brick porch at the back of the house, she peeked through the Dutch door into the kitchen. She could see a blue flowered china plate on which five freshly baked oatmeal cookies awaited her. Folded under it, there was a note on a small scrap of paper.

After opening the icebox door, she pulled out a cream-top milk bottle by its narrow middle, shaking it to mix the rich cream into the skim below, then poured it into a cool glass tumbler.

The best part of her daily routine was reading the message between sips and nibbles. Papa often polished a copper penny and taped it to the note just below where he had scrawled, "To H.A.L.D.W.W.L.," which meant, "To Henrietta Annette Lawrence Dear Whom We Love." Whatever the origin of this custom, Hetty enjoyed it. The rest of the message might be a riddle, a quotation, or something to convey affection.

She read the note:

"The farmer must transport a goat, a wolf and a bale of hay across the river in a rowboat. How must he do it to prevent the wolf from devouring the goat, and the goat from eating the hay?"

Hetty put it in her pocket to consider later. She ran upstairs to her bedroom and opened the window.

Before the Lawrence family had finished settling in their home, Hetty and her father worked together to build a tree house she could reach by crawling out her bedroom window. They spent hours at the basement workbench, whittling little hooks and knobs to look like squirrel tails. And to cover the floor of the little hut, Mother helped Hetty weave a grass mat edged with plaid ribbons. She had hoped Hetty might bring a friend home after school to see it. It seemed the perfect place for twelve-year-old girls to enjoy milk and cookies and talk about the school day the way she had done at that age.

Hetty loosened the strap around her books, resolving to begin her homework. However, after crawling out through the window, she realized she had left the books back on the bed. If the books should levitate and magically follow her to the tree house on their own, Hetty would absolutely, positively see it as a sign that she was supposed to do her homework right now.

She waited dutifully, but when the books had not delivered themselves to her side within a respectable length of time, there was nothing to prevent her from making other plans. Besides, it would be several hours before her parents would drive up the hill in their new 1949 Studebaker. She could still do her homework after that. Now she was free to go see Hannah.

Hetty gazed out over the deep woods and thought of how she had discovered Hannah, the giant oak tree, shortly after they had moved near the new school. Her love for Hannah eased the loneliness she might have otherwise felt in this unfamiliar place. Hetty shared many of her most personal thoughts with Hannah, and she spent many hours reading on her broad horizontal limbs. High among the leaves, Hetty often lost all awareness of time.

Hannah

It was a woodpecker drumming on a hollow tree that had first drawn Hetty into the forest. After she had waded for some time through tangled underbrush in a broad ravine, the confusion of echoes she was following seemed to come from everywhere. Hetty had no idea where she had been, or even whether she had doubled back over her own steps. She found herself on a narrow path made by the paws of many unseen creatures. The route meandered through the dark underbrush until it led her to the edge of the shadows.

There was a whirring of wings, then stillness broken only by the beating of her heart. Or was that really what she heard? A faint rustle now and again made her halt, holding her breath to hear what or who could be watching nearby. She carefully skirted a cluster of fiddlehead ferns and reached forward to sweep aside a barrier of foliage. Suddenly she fell forward and found herself face down on the ground, her hands digging into a soft carpet of leaves.

Her eyes opened to reveal an enchanted clearing, dominated by an immense tree. Years had woven a network of vines that clung to one side of its trunk. Like a tangle of ropes, they heaved up from under the brittle leaves of the forest floor, extending high into the canopy. She slowly inhaled their sweet scent and blinked at the brightness. Hetty feared what she was seeing was only imagined, and the magnificent sight might disappear just as suddenly as she had found it.

The raucous call of a blue jay signaled that all was real. Her left boot had come off when a root snagged her toe.

Turning onto her back, Hetty began to laugh. Above her, the branches seemed to sway in response to her obvious pleasure. She gazed up in wonder at the height and spread of the great oak. The light from the sun was still dancing through the leaves of the upper limbs. With a boot in one hand, she approached to press the open palm of the other against the rough bark.

With this solemn ceremony, I christen thee "Hannah." Actually, I don't have a really true ceremony in mind, but if we can be best friends, I promise I will absolutely, positively never tell anyone about you. I think you must be very old and very, very important, and on the occasion of our ceremony, I hereby bequeath to you this token of grave importance. It's a brand new 1950 penny. Actually, I should have brought a streetcar token. We can't use them now anyway since we moved. That would have been really good to be using a token for a token!

I won't be swearing to anything. Papa says he gets his fill of swearing when he goes to court. That's because he's an attorney.

I wish Mother and Papa could see you, too. But here's the way it is: if they happen to decide they don't want me coming this far into the woods, I couldn't keep my pledge to be your best friend any more. And Papa says whether or not people can keep promises tells a lot about their character.

Papa isn't much of a tree climber, anyway. Neither is Mother. Papa's leg was wounded by an ax when he was fighting fires in the Forest Service. He had two really good buddies. The one named Leaf even saved Papa's life, and Mother limps too because she had polio when she was little. Papa says they were absolutely, positively meant for each other, since they can run a perfect three-legged race.

Melinda and Louisa aren't allowed to come in the woods.
I heard them say so in biology class. The others said it's scary
in here, and that lots of strange things happen in the forest. But
if the woods really are haunted, I know you will be my Protec-
tor. It looks really comfortable up there on your broadest branch
where we can be together and talk.

Hetty took the penny from the note, wedged it into a
crevice of the bark, and considered a variation on the riddle.

A girl has to carry a cookie, a glass of milk and a book up
a tree. The girl can't carry both the cookie and the milk unless
she puts it—no, wait. It would dissolve in the milk—and no, it
won't work to fold the cookie in the pages— Actually, if she eats
the cookie, then technically, she has carried it up the tree, even if
it is in her tummy.

Inky Begins With P

Both Hetty's parents seemed fearless to her, but in different ways.
Neither Mother nor Papa feared wild or unknown places. And
like her parents, Hetty felt at home in the woods. It surprised
them that she was afraid of the dark. She had also been afraid of
dogs when she was younger, but to help Hetty get over it, they
had brought home a gentle female from the dog pound. She
was completely black. Hetty gave her the name Pinky, which
was actually inky, except for starting with a "P."

Curled up in the shadows, Pinky had been hard to see. All
too often someone stepped on one of her paws. It was almost
instinctive to apologize to Pinky and try to comfort the poor
thing after such accidents. However, it was pitiful the way she

would cower under the hand that stroked her, as if she thought some punishment had been intended and there was more to come.

As they couldn't use words to explain things to a dog, they settled on a better way to handle it. When Pinky yelped in pain, they would do something nice for her. Papa might put on his liveliest grin and say, "Go get your ball, Pinky!" The exciting invitation always worked. Pinky would completely forget to limp. With her squeak-ball in her mouth, she would race for the door to play with her best friend.

Hetty watched and wondered. The questions she collected were always saved for bedtime.

"Papa, how can you tell what Pinky's thinking? Is Pinky old in dog years?

Why is it scary at night, even when the lights are on? How old do trees get?"

The Defective Heart

Hetty was born with a defective heart. With the slightest activity she would become very tired and pale. For years nothing could be done for such patients except to keep them warm and comfortable. But her parents wanted her to live as normal a life as possible.

"She'll never feel independent if we are watching her every minute," Papa had said, "so we must encourage her to do the things she can."

When Hetty was seven years old, the doctor told her parents about a hospital in Boston where heart operations were being performed. As he thought it could be more dangerous to do nothing, the decision was made to take her there for surgery.

Hetty had become somewhat aware of the risk to her life. The night before they left, her mother tucked the covers around Hetty, and Papa smoothed back her hair. Hetty had just one question. "What is it like, Papa, going to Heaven?"

"It would be a good thing to talk about another time, Hetty. We'll be getting up very early," Papa answered. After he went downstairs, Hetty heard him honk his nose. Every time he blew it, his nose made an impressive honking sound.

Hetty's parents often said, "Worry is like a rocking chair. It gives you something to do, but it gets you nowhere." Even so, Dan and Dora Lawrence both spent that night worrying about their daughter's surgery. Unable to sleep, Dan composed a poem before morning.

Just as the ocean was beginning to reflect the morning sun, Mother awakened Hetty by singing the jingle from a radio show in her off-key warble.

When Hetty followed the scent of sizzling bacon downstairs to the kitchen, she found an envelope peeking out from under her bowl of Cream of Wheat. Inside the envelope was a soft handkerchief with delicate embroidery and a note that read, "To our Hetty. We hope this handkerchief will bring you good luck. Love, Mother and Papa."

Even after the operation, there were many more sleepless nights. Finally, to their great relief, it was confirmed that Hetty was out of danger. Her heart would mend. Before Hetty left the hospital, she found a bright penny on her breakfast tray, taped to a sheet of stationery. Below it, there was a message from Papa:

Dear Hetty,

I've thought a lot about your question. I'm glad you don't need to know about Heaven just yet. Here is what I think, anyway.

WHAT IS IT LIKE, PAPA, GOING TO HEAVEN?

What is it like, Papa, going to Heaven?
    I know I'm very ill.
What if I die while I'm only seven,
    To lie forever still?

Someone who loves you will carry you home
    To the place where you belong
Gently cradled in His arms,
    All to an angel song.

He'll make you well with the power of love,
    And touch your cheek like me.
You'll fly with Him among the stars;
    That's how Heaven will be.

                All my love,
                Papa XOXO

CHAPTER TWO

Unattached Heads

During the years Hetty had been unable to attend school, she thrived on the excitement of learning at home. Hetty's inborn enthusiasm might have been enough to propel her through the rigorous learning program, but there were additional advantages that encouraged her to excel. She was influenced by Papa's broad vocabulary in a wide range of subjects and her mother's appetite for great literature.

Her parents had been with her most of the time, and there was little contact with others. After the doctor pronounced her to be perfectly healthy, the routines of daily life were suddenly turned upside down and a big adjustment became necessary. She had seldom before seen such large numbers of strange faces as those she confronted on her first day of school.

That night, Hetty dreamed she was floating in the ocean. There were dozens of smiling and talking heads bobbing up and down around her and all of them appeared quite complete and self-contained, without bodies.

In her dream Hetty was given the assignment of putting nametags on all of the heads. She was supposed to match the color of the tag to the eyeball colors, but the heads kept floating away before she was able to attach the proper labels.

To add to the difficulty, the most charming faces could boast a different color for each eye. With one blink, either eye could change its colors like scenes behind a stage curtain. Hetty was very glad to feel relieved of the responsibility by the ringing of her alarm clock.

At breakfast her Mother said, "I'm not surprised you dreamed the way you did. There must be many people you're trying to keep straight at school."

Haxton Academy

Hetty's parents had been very glad to find such an excellent school for girls. The Haxton Country Academy met in what was once a very large old home with graceful wood-paneled corridors and squeaky floorboards of sweet-smelling oak. With only ten girls to a class, they hoped twelve-year-old Hetty might receive the necessary attention.

They had been especially pleased to hear wonderful reports about the new headmistress who had also just come to the school. Hetty learned that Mrs. Fairburn had been teaching English in a large town for years. She accepted the new position only after the recent death of her husband and moved quietly into a cottage near the woods.

In order to be closer to this new school for Hetty's sake, the Lawrence family had found it necessary to move from some distance away. They were pleased to find a small house on an elevated plot from which the ocean was visible. In the other direction, it overlooked a thick forest.

Dan and Dora had mistakenly assumed the unspoiled forestland would attract other families with children. They were soon disappointed to learn this was not the case; however, Hetty was content to have the woods all to herself. Besides, if they had not moved to this new location, she would never have discovered Hannah. The giant tree had quickly become her dearest friend.

Although Hetty felt comfortable in the company of her parents, she was more reserved around other people. When the teacher expected her to speak aloud, she would feel the heat creeping up her neck until her cheeks became quite pink, and she would have to lower her eyes and run her fingers over the letters on her handkerchief.

Daniel and Dora had thought she would soon outgrow her shyness, but instead, she created a world of daydreams, which caused her to withdraw further. If only she could pay attention in class, Hetty might have been a better student; however, even the most trivial things diverted her thoughts.

The Penalty for Daydreaming

During French class one afternoon, Hetty was listening to the sparrows in the tree outside the classroom window. She was supposed to be studying a grammar section called *"Antoine à l'École,"* but her mind had carried her to a sunny perch on Hannah's broad horizontal trunk.

"Oh, Annette…my beloved Annette! The way you toss your hair… It makes me wild with desire!
"Desire, Antoine?"

"Indeed, my dear one. Your curls capture the sun like the foam of a breaking wave, and I long to escape to the wild open sea."

"To the sea, Antoine?"

"Yes, my darling, and I can hear the rapturous cry of a seagull soaring overhead."

As their fingertips touched tenderly, Hetty thought of the immense dropping a gull had once left on Papa's windshield.

"I don't think I want him to kiss me," she mused. "I don't know what people do with their noses; they must get in the way."

"Antoine, we mustn't. We dasn't."

"Dasn't? That's not even a word, my love."

"Yes, it is."

"Is not."

"Is too."

"Is not."

"Don't you even know about archaic words, dear Antoine?"

"Oh! I wish I was smart like you, Annette."

Slowly she raised her arms to spread a gossamer cape, tossing her hair in the beams of the golden sun for one last time. Her mysterious silence maddened and enthralled him. He watched as she floated gracefully from her perch, piercing the frothy billows below with her dainty toes. Inconsolable, he watched his beloved disappear forever from his life, as her name burned in his anguished heart.

"Annette! Annette!"

"Annette! Henrietta Annette Lawrence!" Madame du Pré shrieked, "We're on number fourteen, and it's your turn." Since Hetty had failed to notice her teacher's repeated de-

Her name burned in his anguished heart.

mands for attention, the angry French teacher marched her across the hall toward Mrs. Fairburn's office. The other students tried not to stare as the new girl passed, the heels of her father's oversized boots clunking along the floor and leather shoelaces trailing behind her.

After a brief explanation to Mrs. Fairburn that included flapping her pointy elbows, Madame du Pré left Hetty with the headmistress and stormed back to the classroom.

Lady Fairburn

The new headmistress could see that Hetty was humiliated by the laughter of the other students. She closed the door against the sound and consulted her files to see what she could learn about the frightened girl. After just a brief glance at the papers and at Hetty, Mrs. Fairburn knew she needed time to think through what she had just discovered. She turned her face to the window. Hetty must not be allowed to see that she was startled.

After a long silence, she turned her gray eyes to study Hetty. "What is it you want to learn? Tell me what makes you happy, Hetty Anne," she asked.

"I...I'm....Well...." whispered Hetty. She twisted her handkerchief then felt for the "H.A.L." embroidered on it. The handkerchief had been hers since birth. It was absolutely and positively her most treasured possession, but she hadn't known about it until after her heart operation at the age of seven. Mother said it was Hardanger embroidery on white linen.

"There are many girls who come here to learn. Is that why you have come here?" Mrs. Fairburn paused and smiled. "Would you prefer to answer my question in a letter?"

She hadn't mentioned the classroom incident, and her voice was kind. Hetty was remembering the time she had thought a glass she held contained buttermilk. But when she put it to her lips, it turned out to be a sweet vanilla milkshake.

Mrs. Fairburn's every word was pronounced with lovely precision, as if she had invented each individual syllable herself, and felt some ongoing responsibility toward them all. Hetty thought it would be absolutely, positively heavenly to be able to talk just like her someday.

"My dear and honored Lady Fairburn: O that the sacred beauty of our language might be preserved! I am but thy humble servant, and yet in me, you have found a kindred spirit! The sloppy English people use these days is scandalous, do you not think?

"Also, I might mention that I saw a really, really annoying sign, that says, "Nasty Tasty." Mother says it's supposed to say "Hasty Tasty," but someone just got lazy the way they crossed the "H." I would never eat there, for sure!

"Anyway, like I was saying, it doth behoove me to pledge my troth, or whatever one doth, to be thy standard bearer."

"Ah, yes, Hetty Anne. These are times when one must pledge one's troth, mustn't one?"

"Indeed one must. Actually, if you have a talisman, Lady Fairburn — or something akin to a talisman, I shall be honored to guard it in my bosom."

Hetty climbed, cradling Lady Fairburn's sacred object, until she reached a cavity high in the tree. Her tree, Hannah, would keep the secret in her heart.

Hetty thought of the way the glee club teacher had made them articulate the word "boozum," over and over. How embarrassing.

She looked at the headmistress and nodded, to indicate she would write a letter. After lunch, she put it under Mrs. Fairburn's door.

Dear Mrs. Fairburn,

WHAT I WANT TO LEARN

I. To sound good when I talk.
II. Some really great words, so I can beat my papa at Scrabble.
III. To sew like my mother (Not at school).
IV. No math for heaven's sake! I only need it when Papa and I are building things I have to measure.
V. How to live like Swiss Family Robinson, my very favorite story ever!
VI. LOTS of things I will think of later.

Love From Your Friend,
Miss Henrietta Annette Lawrence

Violence is Not Boring

The other girls would sometimes ask Hetty, "Didn't you get bored at home?"

She did not. There were lots of interesting things Hetty remembered about those times. In fact those earlier years had actually been full of adventure. Papa had helped her build a crystal set with a long barbed-wire antenna. It kind of worked. At least she could hear a few radio programs in the backyard.

Mother had taught her to sew. The blue flowered nightgown she made was pretty enough to be worth repairing and patching for many years. Hetty put ten pockets up and down the front of it so she could gather nuts or leaves to identify, and because she never knew when she might need to keep a piece of chalk, a rubber band or a paperclip within reach. Also, her handkerchief had to be available at all times, in case her fingers needed to feel for the initials embroidered on it.

Hetty had loved gathering wild asparagus and learning the names of the flowers and trees. If her mouth felt furry after eating wild persimmons, she brushed her teeth with the crushed end of a sassafras twig. She boiled acorns, roasting and pounding them to make flour. No, she hadn't been bored.

She thought back to the day when she had been resting in the backyard sun, completely unaware of a drama that was about to take place. The event became ever more real as Hetty relived it in her mind:

They watched as a cone-shaped pit opened mysteriously in the earth. A villainous monster was spewing sand as it raged and seethed in the underworld. Daniel put his arm protectively around his beloved wife and daughter. In horror, they witnessed the approach of a hapless victim nearing the steep slope of the hole. Falling over the ridge, he slipped closer and closer to his fate. Even as he struggled for his very life, the quicksand gave way, sucking him down, down, down. The monster heaved ferociously from his underground lair to launch his final attack. Plunging his hollow mandibles through the quicksand, he sucked the insides out of the helpless victim. The hideous jaws of death had drawn the ant to its doom. Daniel comforted his terrified family, reassuring them that insects such as this ant lion would never take over the world.

No, Hetty had not been bored.

Ice Cream Trouble

Dan and Dora had said, "You learned a lot while you were at home, and now it's going to be a big change for you, learning at school instead." They were right. It was a big change, and sometimes Hetty needed to tell her tree all about it.

Hi, Hannah. Guess what happened at lunch. Lots of times I sit with Sue, 'cause she's nice. And besides, she looked kind of lonely today. I went over to sit with her, because the girl next to her moved to sit by someone else. I didn't know why, but it was because Sue's breath was really, really awful today. I was afraid I'd throw up. It was like rotten fish or dog food or something, but I stayed there because I thought it would hurt her feelings if I moved.

Anyway, Miss Altoona was watching over our table. She's the one that monitors the study hall, and she can actually see inside our brains. She walks around between desks with her little book and a red pencil, and puts a mark in it every time she even suspects we're thinking about something besides our homework, for fear we won't be accepted at Radcliffe and it would be her fault. Then if we get too many marks, we get sent to the headmistress.

Anyway, my ice cream was so cold it hurt my head and right here behind my throat, so I stirred it to make it smooth and melty. Miss Altoona kept looking our way, and then she got up and came around behind me and tapped me on the shoulder. She had me follow her into the hall, and then we just stood there for the longest time.

What she did not say was, "You poor child, you may trade seats with me. You have been ever so brave, and now it is only fair that I endure Sue's horrible breath for the remainder of the meal." What she did say was, "I would like you to reflect on the offensive nature of your actions."

I reflected and reflected. I reflected real hard, since I really like Miss Fairburn, and I didn't want to go to her office and have her find out I wasn't nice and that I wouldn't deserve to go to Radcliffe.

I guess Miss Altoona could tell I'd still be reflecting all through next summer vacation, or at least long enough for her ice cream to melt, so she finally told me what I'd done. She said, "Nice young ladies don't stir their ice cream." The way she said it, I could tell it was a mortal sin. Absolutely the mortalest. Even worse than chewing gum.

One thing Papa says is that rules usually make sense if they're made by people we trust. I just have to figure out what they are. Papa says jails are full of people who don't follow rules.

But here's what I think: There ought to be a law that if your breath is so bad that it wilts the flowers in the centerpiece, you shouldn't be allowed to exhale that day.

CHAPTER THREE

Miss Altoona and the PTA

The Lawrences had hoped to learn more about Hetty's school life by going to their first parent-teacher conference. However, as Dan and Dora mingled with the teachers, for the most part they heard what they had been expecting to hear.

"She's very quiet."

"What can we do to help her?"

"Her test scores are almost perfect."

"Her thoughts are miles away."

The meeting began with Mrs. Fairburn's warm welcome. The new headmistress introduced herself briefly in a manner they would all remember. She smiled with her large gray eyes, almost as if she already knew each one of them well and would forever be generous in her judgment of them.

As questions and answers were exchanged, there was a general pleasant sentiment that pervaded the room. The fragrance of aging boxwood at the entrance joined the scent of the worn oak floors within, to speak of a long history of stability. The very best of its history seemed certain to repeat itself in this place.

Miss Altoona had come to the meeting especially to see Hetty's parents. "I wasn't actually scheduled to come tonight," she explained, "but I was hoping to talk to you about Hetty. She is noticeably kind to the other girls, and thoughtful in spite of her shyness. Even in small ways, she is considerate of people's feelings."

"I appreciate your telling us," Dora replied.

"I've been concerned about how abrupt I was with her yesterday," Miss Altoona continued.

"We weren't aware...." Dan began.

Miss Altoona breathed deeply, and began again. "The way she was eating was conspicuous, but she didn't seem to be aware of the other girls watching her, and how her manners looked. I had to get her away from the table quickly, before anyone else noticed."

"Oh dear. It's really never occurred to us to...." Dan replied.

"I want her good qualities to be appreciated by the other girls, but until Hetty learns what looks offensive or inappropriate to others, that won't happen. It's something I hope we can help her with here at Haxton."

"We haven't...that is, we should have thought about preparing her..." stammered Dora.

A Diamond in Combat Boots

"If I may continue to be direct," Miss Altoona continued apologetically, "there is just one other thing you should know; there are not any other girls wearing combat boots to school. We have delayed telling her to wear the uniform shoes, because her boots seem so important to her."

Dan and Dora glanced at each other. Hetty was their greatest treasure! They both felt they were to blame for her classmates viewing her differently.

"Hetty is a diamond in the rough," Miss Altoona emphasized, "and diamonds need polishing."

During the rest of the meeting, and later as they were driving home, the Lawrences each silently pondered Hetty's future. Dora thought of the grace and warmth of Mrs. Fairburn, and hoped that Hetty could learn from her example. "Dan, haven't we met the headmistress somewhere before?"

"No, I'm sure I would have remembered her, Dorie."

Dan glanced at his wife. He knew Dora had wanted to be a mother as long as she could remember. In preschool, she had tried singing "Rock-a-bye Baby" to a hammer, or just about anything that could be wrapped in a baby blanket. Even today almost everything about Dora was small in scale, except her heart. She smiled at him with her miniature teeth, and straightened her small white collar with her tiny hands. In the approaching headlights, he admired her unmanageable wisps of hair. She wore a braid wrapped around her head to contain them, but a number of them had escaped hours ago.

"Dorie will know what to do about Hetty," he thought.

She did. At least she hoped so. On her next trip to the library, she would get the book *Etiquette* by Emily Post, unless Miss Reed, the librarian, could suggest a better one. Dora felt confident Hetty would read it, because she had read almost every book her mother brought home.

In the Forest Service

Dan was deep in his own worried thoughts. He was secretly
pleased that Hetty wanted to wear his Forest Service boots
made by White's Boot Company, and that her feet were long
enough to fit them if she wore thick stockings. He was flat-
tered by his daughter's affection for him, and pleased with the
interests they shared.

Hetty often asked him about the Forest Service. Dan
tried to recall one of their conversations. There was one thing
in particular he had told her that worried him in light of what
Miss Altoona had said. It concerned a tradition that Zack,
Leaf, and he had started. His thoughts went back to an evening meal with the whole crew the first year the three of them
had worked together.

Polite Night, Rude Night

*"Pass the corn," demanded Pete. "Hey, Knothead, pass the stupid
corn!" he repeated. Knothead shoved the corn down the table.*

*Buff stood to reach a long arm way down the table, hoping
to stab the largest steak with his knife. Johnson raced to get there
first. Winning the slab of meat, Johnson waved it high overhead
on his fork.*

"More meat, Gret!" someone yelled to the cook.

*That made Greta mad as a hornet. They figured that out
right away, when she started banging pans. She stormed out of
the kitchen, pointing and jabbing her trigger finger toward the of-
fenders.*

*"You highfalutin college guys....When you get out here in the
woods, you don't think it matters how you act. Well, it does, same
as everywhere. So shape up, or I'm out of here!" She put her hands*

on her hips. "And it wouldn't kill you to say please and thank you," she snorted.

At breakfast, Leaf said, "Greta wasn't too crazy about our manners at dinner last night."

Pete swore. "What kinda lousy stuff does she want us to do anyway? Bet she'll want us to talk all fancy," he said.

"Naw, come on, guys," Speedy drawled pitifully.

"We owe her something after last night," said Zack. "She's the reason we get good food. If it weren't for her, we'd be out picking nuts and berries."

They remembered the steaks and were convinced.

"Okay, guys, tonight's Polite Night," Zack announced.

Greta was delighted to see an orderly line waiting patiently, when she put out the food. The week before, someone had tried to weasel his way to the front of the line, but the others taught him a lesson. They had hoisted him overhead and passed him the length of the line, tossing him off the back at the end. He wouldn't be trying that again anytime soon.

The first in line was Knothead. He doffed his cap to reveal a sweaty head of matted hair. "Good evening, Miss Greta. What a pleasure to see you. Man, what a divine repast! You whip it up all by yourself?"

"You know I did," she laughed.

She looked over the entire crew: the peeling sunburns, the muscles bursting to keep moving, and restless energy suited to the wilderness. Greta returned their good-natured grins. If there was one word to describe the men, "dainty" was not it. There were the usual ill-fitting tee shirts with rips and burns, but tonight, especially for her, there was a necktie hanging down the front of each of their broad chests. They were not a bad lot.

No sooner had they arranged themselves at the benches, than they began to out-polite each other.

"Oh, kind Sir, may I trouble you for a second serviette? I could use one for my upper lip as well," said Dan.

"With pleasure," answered Zack. "Perhaps I could offer you a portion of cornbread?"

"After you."

"Au contraire, my good man, after you."

"This is real palatable cuisine, Greta," said Speedy.

"Yeah," Pete grunted.

"Every morsel is delectable," Johnson interjected.

"Yeah, real terrific morsels," added Pete. "Can I kindly have some more stew morsels?"

"We are much obliged for the real succulent grub, Greta."

Greta finally threw herself into the act with a clumsy curtsy and added, "Many thanks, gentlemen!"

For the most part, the gentlemen themselves had considered Polite Night rather successful, yet a certain basic earthy need had been left unsatisfied. A few days later, Dan, Leaf and Zack went to Greta on a delicate mission, representing the whole crew.

Leaf began, "We appreciate your patience and hope you will understand… The problem is we wouldn't want to offend you, so if you could possibly plan to be away… or go to town some night this week, after you've set out the food. It looks like enthusiasm is building for… for a…"

"Rude Night," Zack inserted.

"We'll be sure and clean up before you get back," Dan volunteered.

Greta accepted the inevitable.

"Begging your pardon, I do believe I spy the mashed potatoes in your neck of the woods. Would you be so kind as to deliver them in my direction, henceforth?" Zack requested.

Buff plopped his hand into the mashed potatoes, lifting a large scoop. He squished it through his knobby knuckles in the general location of Zack's tin plate upon which it might have landed, if Johnson hadn't snatched the plate first.

"How genteel," crowed Knothead.

"Might I trouble you for some peas?" Dan asked.

"Certainly, but hark! Didn't Zack make a request for something down his neck? Gravy, I presume?"

"Indeed he did."

"Yeah," drawled Speedy, with one eye gleaming at the gravy bowl.

Zack loaded his spoon with peas, and flipped them toward an open mouth across from him.

A grin spread across Knothead's face. "Now, there's manners!"

"Yeah, real manners," Pete chortled.

"Let's hear it for manners!" Johnson cheered. There was general loud whooping and table pounding in support of the new balance their etiquette had attained.

"I perceive that the lemonade receptacle is now empty," observed Dan, who was secretly relieved that it was no longer available to be poured over anyone.

Buff had just poured the last of the lemonade into his own tin cup before he went off to the privy. So no one else would want his precious lemonade while he was gone, he had propped a note against it that said, "I spit in this."

Before Buff's return, Dan scrawled, "So did I," at the bot-

tom of the note.

Pete burped and scratched.

"In China," Leaf said, "burping is actually polite. It's a compliment to the chef."

"No lie!" Johnson exclaimed. "Then we better see who can pay the biggest compliment."

"You're on," said Leaf. "The winner gets to pick who cleans up."

Leaf won the belching contest by a landslide, but he joined the entire crew in scrubbing down the cook shack and all around the tables. When Dan organized the cleaning process into a relay race complete with human mops, everyone thought the cleaning was part of the entertainment.

Then they lined up for showers in what they called the Gypsy Wagon, to remove the potatoes and gravy that caked their hair. When Greta returned, she could detect no trace of Rude Night.

"Oh, Dorie...I wish I hadn't told Hetty about Rude Night," Dan moaned.

Library Phobia

Dora had a gift for choosing just the right books at the library. Even so, she always invited Hetty to go along with her, hoping it would give her daughter experience talking with people. She would also be able to see how useful and fun a library card would be. Dora would say, "Mrs. Ash's little girl is a lot younger than you are, and she has her own library card. Wouldn't you like to get acquainted with the librarian, dear? Marian Reed is a good friend of mine. She feels like she already knows you, since she's been helping me choose books you would like."

Here's the way it is: Mother doesn't realize that probably the librarian will be sitting behind a huge desk and ask me lots of questions with her teeth clenched, and she'll use words like matriculate, and arbitrate, and I bet she'll say if I want a card I have to tell her stuff I don't know like the serial number from the carburetor of our car, and when she says everyone else knows the serial number of their carburetor but me, all the children with library cards will whisper and laugh behind their hands, and I'll have to pretend I have an important appointment so I can leave before I throw up.

Since it would take me too long to explain all this to Mother, I'll just say, "Um, well, I don't know," a few times until she kisses me goodbye. Besides, she couldn't possibly understand; she's not afraid to hypotenuse her way around anywhere.

Hetty read the library book about etiquette when her mother brought it to her. The overview on showing thoughtfulness was helpful, and she was also fascinated by how to eat oysters, use fingerbowls, and address people she thought were too important to see except in parades. When the time came to return the book, Hetty was reluctant to give it up, so Dan bought her a copy of her own. Inside the cover, he wrote, "For purposes of gilding the lily."

CHAPTER FOUR

Dora's Birthday

For her mother's birthday Hetty had whittled a whistle that looked like a bird. In art class, all the drawings she did were for Mother's birthday card. Hetty kept in mind the things she and Papa had done for her every year.

He always gives her pink roses that she pretends she wasn't expecting. I think there's time to do my math before I set the table, and I'll make her a paper crown. Maybe Papa will let me be the one who turns on the Victrola this year, but he'll have to pick the best record, and they'll dance, and she'll be all flirty with him.

She always says stuff like, "Oh, Daniel! My dance card is absolutely full, but I'd much rather dance with you!" And she'll pretend to cross out a whole bunch of names. They'd all be famous princes and football players and really handsome movie-star-looking men who, if they were real, would for sure be absolutely and positively broken-hearted, if not worse.

Hetty envisioned a long tragic line of men waiting to be admitted to a monastery.

And Mother will say, "This is the most fun ever! Hetty, did you know I thought your father liked to dance? That was before we were married."

And Papa will say, "It was the only way I could put my arms around Dorie in those days."

Then we'll all dance together with me stepping on their toes and laughing, and I'll dish up the ice cream, and I've made enough confetti to sprinkle around our best plates, and Papa will lay a fire and we'll play Scrabble, then Mother will say it was the best day ever and kiss me about a million times, and she'll kiss Papa another million times when they don't think I'm watching.

I guess they don't know they're old. But they're not too limpy.

That same afternoon after school, Melinda asked Hetty, "Can you come over? I hope you can, because you're not boring or anything. Some people talk, talk, talk all the time; I'm glad you're not like that. My dad can take you home after."

Upstairs in the Morganthals' house, after Melinda had led Hetty up the long curved stairway, she stopped at an open door. "That's my brother," she said, almost the way she would if she were showing off a new sailboat. "He can't get his crystal set working." She pulled Hetty into the opening. "This is Hetty."

A boy with a thatch of dark hair stood up as she appeared.

Hetty had seen how men stood up when her mother walked into a room. She reached out her hand like her Emily Post book said to do, and he took her hand. "I'm Morgan," he said.

The crystal set had caught Hetty's attention right away, and she inspected it more closely.

"Hetty's made one," volunteered Melinda.

"Well...with my Papa," said Hetty. "Maybe you need a longer antenna?"

Hetty noticed Morgan had a black eye, and wondered if he had gotten in a fight at school, or just how it had happened.

I wonder if he got wounded while defending the honor of a damsel in distress, or if someone picked a fight with him because they wanted him to cheat on a test and he wouldn't. Maybe he walked into a wall.

I hope it'll turn out like in the cartoons. Bugs Bunny is always having disasters like getting squashed flat as a pancake, but when it's time to move on with the story, you hear "Boinnng!" and suddenly it looks as if nothing had happened to him.

"What did you use for an antenna?" Morgan asked.

"We used our fence," Hetty answered.

"That's clever!" he grinned. "That is a long one."

In Melinda's room, Hetty marveled at the mural of a circus scene with an ocean and a boardwalk included, covering the entire wall behind a high bed. The canopy of the bed was striped with all the colors of cotton candy, and it looped down from the high ceiling in swags and tassels. The bed could be reached by climbing up one of two sets of little pink and white wrought iron steps.

Hetty could hardly believe she was a guest there, talking with the most popular girl in the school ever! Hetty's main contribution was to listen and smile, because whenever Melinda asked a question, she would provide the answer herself.

Hetty tried to look interested in everything Melinda was saying, but she kept thinking of Mother. It seemed like she listened for a very long time.

"You know why I don't go in these woods?" asked Melinda. "I heard about this guy whose mother died, and he kept her in the closet for years and years and he dressed like he was her, and he would go every month and collect the money like his mother used to get from the government. When they caught him they found his mother, and she had turned into a mummy. I'm not lying. And her hair kept growing after she was dead. Her fingernails did too." Melinda made scary cat claws with her hands.

"I'll tell you a secret: There's this really strange man who lives in the woods, and it's probably him, doing the very same thing again! Honest." Melinda crossed her heart. Hetty wondered how many times this strange man could get away with the same crime.

She was thinking of the birthday card she had made for Mother. She carefully brought it out to show Melinda, because after all, they were good friends now, what with having secrets and all.

"You're a real good artist!" Melinda smiled at Hetty, as if to say, "You might be famous like Leonardo da Vinci some day."

Then Melinda took a red crayon from her pocket. "I like to draw, too. Here is some champagne for your mother." And she drew a drink with bubbles billowing out all over. On the inside, under Hetty's best drawing, she wrote, "Happy Birthday. Don't have TOO much fun!!! Love, Me, Linda."

Hetty inspected the card and felt a little sick to her stomach. "I better go," she stammered.

"Please stay a little longer. Please, please, please!" Melinda begged, using one of her more tragic faces. "When my parents get home at night, they don't usually feel too good," she added.

Soon they heard car tires on the gravel of the driveway. Two people stumbled through the dark and into the back door of the house. Doors slammed downstairs, and then there was no sound.

Hetty quickly said a quiet goodbye, but Melinda didn't notice. She had climbed into her canopy bed with all her clothes on and pulled a peach satin and lace comforter up over her head. Hetty decided Melinda was afraid of something. Probably the dark.

After silently closing the heavy front door behind her, Hetty began to run along the street. The tears came. After several miles, Papa's big boots rubbed her heel sore and her books became very heavy.

I wonder what Mother and Papa are thinking about me. I hope they didn't notice how I wasn't there. I hope maybe they started to look at the paper to see who President Truman had invited to the White House for dinner and then read all through dinnertime and fell asleep on the couch with their glasses on their noses and didn't even remember the birthday, or how I was supposed to be there.

I could do like the way it worked with Pinky....to do something sort of nice for her. When it's tomorrow, I could say, "Oh, isn't it your birthday?" kind of casually.

Papa was standing at the door waiting. Mother was doing the dishes. They looked very tired.

"Oh, Papa," she sobbed, while he held her tight. "Papa...."

Then Mother took Hetty's face in both her hands, and wiped away the tears with her thumbs. There were no words.

When Hetty was in bed, she realized she had run all those miles without thinking of the darkness. Her thoughts had been of home, where there was love and where a light would be shining.

Mother rubbed her back until she fell asleep.

When they arrived at their desks next morning, Melinda pressed a note into Hetty's hand.

To Hetty,

I'm sorry about last night. Morgan said I shouldn't of pretended I was sleeping. I was just kidding. I didn't hear you go. My parents didn't know you came! Next time we will drive you home I promise! I hope we are still friends! Is your phone number Oliver 3316, because mine is Oliver 2216. I think that is interesting!!!!!

Love,

Me, Linda

Fears

Melinda hadn't simply pretended to be asleep. She was afraid. Hetty was sure of it. High in Hannah, Hetty sat in a spot of sunlight and talked about what it was like to be afraid.

What's scariest is the things you know aren't real. Because you can't make something go away that's not even there.

Like when I cooked a wasp on my play stove. I put it in a saucepan with a lid. The lid had pink zigzags with pictures of pink cars in a row around it. I guess they thought if they painted cars on it, people would buy the cook sets for boys too.

Anyway, I guess the pink decorations were supposed to make it seem like make-believe and so it would be okay. But after I turned on the stove, it didn't seem that way at all. It was buzzing and trying desperately to stay up off the hot bottom of the pan. I was crying, but I was too scared to open the lid, in case he got out and was stronger and more ferocious than when I put him in there, and he'd come get me. Then it was too late because the buzzing stopped.

I think I made up an excuse for myself that the lid was too hot to touch, or I couldn't see anything to lift it up with. I'm not sure anymore if I made that part up or not.

I used to look in the drain when I was in the shower, but I don't do that any more because the wasp reaches its skinny thread-like legs up through the slats that look like jail bars. It wants to pull me down in the dark drain with hairs in it.

After it was dead, I never opened the lid. I couldn't tell Mother and Papa what I'd done, and why the wasp that wasn't really there kept being under my bed. Sometimes it was so big and ferocious that I couldn't even roll over, or else its black and yellow abdomen would start to quiver like it was planning to get more pumped up with poison.

Then later on, a really amazing thing happened. I saw this beautiful silver wasp nest that was absolutely and positively perfect. I watched the wasps go in and out and I told them how beautiful their house was. I didn't tell them what I'd done, but it was like they knew anyway, or they'd forgotten, and I was meant to see it so I wouldn't have nightmares anymore. They knew I loved watching them make something even clever human beings couldn't make. It seemed like the more I kept watching them, the more they weren't under my bed at night.

I wish I'd opened the lid, even if I'd burned my fingers. Even if it attacked me. That's better than doing something I couldn't tell Papa about. Papa says there isn't anything we do that can't be fixed, and talking about it can be part of fixing it. I guess that's why I'm telling you.

Maybe we can fix whatever scares Melinda. Here's one good thing: she says she and Morgan always stick together, so she has someone to talk to.

Another thing I never told Mother and Papa about, was when we were supposed to take aprons to school. Mother stayed up most of the night and made me a beautiful apron with ruffles. She even embroidered a pocket that looked like a birdhouse with a bluebird peeking out the hole, and when I took it to school, the art teacher said it would be better to just bring an old shirt of my father's to use like a smock. I couldn't tell Mother, so I left it at school.

I couldn't go back without a smock either, so I ran away from home and hid for the whole day. The school must have called them at work, because I saw Papa driving around in the Studebaker looking for me. He looked really old and worried, but I wasn't sure it was because of me, so I stayed hidden behind *a stone wall and didn't know what to do. I went home because I didn't have anything to eat. I would tell them about it now, but it might make them sad to know I couldn't talk to them about it when it first happened.*

I still don't know what to do about things that aren't right or wrong. Like when things are medium right or half wrong, and you can't use math to measure how much of each.

The Librarian

After the Lawrence family had moved to be near Hetty's school, one of the first people Dora met was the librarian. When Dora had first seen her, Marian Reed was behind a large desk, completely engrossed in reading a copy of *Pride and Prejudice*, which she held in her lap. That corner of the room would have been a rather effective hiding place if it hadn't been for the red hair that framed her face and announced her presence.

Dora spoke the name she saw displayed on the desk. She had to repeat it louder a second time before the librarian reluctantly raised her head. Marian's eyes had been lowered for the purpose of reading, but more importantly to prevent unwanted friendly interruptions. All this seemed curious in a person who was there to serve the public.

Marian Reed opened her thick lashes to reveal a pair of large brown eyes. Her expression was at once both thoughtful and lonely. Upon seeing the friendly face across the desk, she found herself immediately drawn to Dora. Marian was unused to trusting people so quickly, while it was in Dora's nature to believe others to be honest and kind. She never thought anyone likely to harm her or to deceive her in any way.

A few days after her birthday, Dora had received a package in the mail with no return address on the outside to indicate who had sent it. She thought it must be a late birthday gift, but it was not. Upon opening the box, she found a note that said:

To Mrs. Lawrence,

The reason I was running in the rain with a briefcase was so somebody would stop and pick me up. I was going to get rid of them and steal their car. You were nice to give me your hus-band's raincoat, so I did not do it. Here is the coat thank you. You should be more careful next time.

Dan was horrified by what might have happened, and asked her to promise never, under any circumstances, to pick up a stranger again. As she tucked a wandering strand of hair in place, she reminded him that everything had turned out all right, and that people were basically good.

Marian heard the story later in Dora's sunny kitchen. She was so amazed to learn of her friend's reaction that she dropped her spoon in the raspberries and cream. Dora's attitude toward the stranger was very different from what her own would have been.

As she and Marian became close, Dora learned why it was difficult for her friend to trust people. Marian's life had been harder than Dora's.

Marian's mother had always claimed she could fix anything with duct tape, but duct tape hadn't been invented in time to fix her marriages. She had taught her daughter it was best to avoid men altogether if she hoped for happiness in this life, so Marian had wanted little to do with men. She felt they might make adequate doorstops, but they couldn't be counted on for anything more complicated than that. Her mother ought to know, because she had married several doorstops.

Marian claimed her stepfathers were always getting misplaced because they wouldn't ask for directions. She hadn't minded their disappearing, with one exception. She had really missed Joey when he left. Joey once peeled a potato in such a long thin strip that it reached all the way to the mail slot from where she was holding it. He had picked up little Marian and danced her around the kitchen afterwards.

Then one day Joey disappeared without saying goodbye, leaving nothing behind him but the potato peeling. For weeks Marian thought he had left it for her as a sign of his affection. Surely he would come back. She had kept it until her mother found it and tossed it out.

Marian's preferred friends were the loving and constant people she found only in books. But when Daniel Lawrence came to the library to pick up some books being held for Hetty, he smiled, and after he honked his nose, he excused himself so cheerfully that Marian could understand why Dora wasn't trying to misplace him.

One evening as she was straightening the library, Marian saw a book by Elizabeth Bibesco lying open on the table. She read these words:

"To others we are not ourselves but performers in their lives cast for a part we do not even know we are playing." Marian thought about Dan and Dora, who didn't even realize the important part they were performing in her life. She hoped to enlarge the role they played, and perhaps to meet Hetty someday as well.

Bridge to the Hideaway

When her parents had first shown Hetty their new home, Papa pointed to the forest, and she was absolutely certain he had called it, "Olive Witch, our forest to enjoy." But the thought came to her one afternoon while she was reading *Ivanhoe* that instead of speaking of the forest, Papa had been referring to the many things within their view. He had said, "…all of which are for us to enjoy." It had taken Hetty a long time to unravel the phrase the way he had said it. A name like "All of Which" would never do for a place of such importance, she reflected, but "Olive Witch" was a perfect name for the forest.

One spring afternoon, Hetty had taken a book into Olive Witch Forest. Leaning against Hannah's trunk, her eyes strayed to an ovenbird weaving its small domed nest. The lady's slippers and Jack-in-the-pulpit would soon be pushing up nearby from the dark soil. The little bird rustled through the dry leaves, and finding a snail, it hopped to the foot of the cliff behind Hannah.

At the base of the cliff there was a boulder that appeared to be heaving itself up from the center of the earth like a giant Titan. Directly above and near the top of the ledge, leaves and branches reached toward the sheer surface, almost completely hiding the hollow from which the boulder had fallen.

Hetty tucked a leaf in her book to keep her place and went around the back of the tree to look up at the hollow space. It would not be large enough to allow her to stand; however, it was more than spacious enough to provide protection in a rainstorm.

The very day she discovered it, Hetty got to work. She gathered some good sturdy branches that had fallen nearby over the winter. There were enough of them to form a bridge from her branch to the hideaway. The vines of honeysuckle and Virginia creeper were plentiful and strong, making ropes and nails unnecessary. Not much would be required of the bridge, as there was such a short distance to be spanned. So in just a few days, Hetty had finished building it.

The cliff cave would make a very pleasant nest. It allowed just enough space for Hetty to stretch her toes to one end and her fingertips to the other. There was a flat place for her books at the back, and room for the treasure box containing Papa's notes. The flowered tablecloth she wasn't really using in her tree house would brighten the space, and she could think of many uses for it.

When she sat at the very front with her legs hanging over the edge, her boots rested with absolute precision upon a little ledge that stretched steeply up to her left. The ledge formed a sort of trail where it reached the cliff at its highest point; however, it was too narrow for her to use safely. After pulling up three spindly weeds, she cleared out a few dry bones cluttering the back. Hetty could picture an archaeopteryx hiding them there a hundred fifty million years ago especially for her to discover.

The floor needed a soft lining, so she descended to search the ground for something that might be suitable. She paused briefly to listen as the wind whispered, almost like a distant violin, then she danced and swirled to the windsong until the crisp leaves underfoot reminded her of the task she had begun.

Gathering leaves in the fullness of her skirt, she made her way up through Hannah's boughs to scatter them on the floor of her new hideaway. This she repeated until she was satisfied that the work was done. Now, whenever she crossed over the bridge from Hannah to her hideaway, Hetty would feel as snug and invisible as an ovenbird in her own nest.

CHAPTER FIVE

Leaf and Zack

With time, Hetty became eager to learn more about outdoor survival, and Dan was pleased to share his knowledge with her. When he had fought fires in the Forest Service, he and his companions were trapped by fires several times. They had lived on blueberries and porcupine meat, so he valued those survival skills. However, there were some painful memories from the fires of that last year that he chose to keep to himself.

The summer of 1938 was an unusual fire season. Violent and widespread fires destroyed much of the nation's forestland. The government urgently requested all firefighters with previous experience to volunteer, so Dora had understood why Dan had to go. He had graduated from law school and passed the bar exam. After returning in the fall, he would open his own law office with Dora as his secretary and begin his life as an attorney.

Upon arriving at the bunkhouse, Dan was hailed by the two friends he had most wanted to see there. He had many memories of Zack and the tall, powerful Leaf Locke, and of sweating and laboring alongside these two companions the previous years.

When Dan first met Leaf Locke, he also learned the reason behind his name. Leaf's mother had been so proud of her Norwegian heritage that she had named him after the Norwegian explorer, Leif Eriksson. The trouble was his name was spelled differently, so people asked questions like, "What kind of tree did you fall from?" His best answer was, "A Norway maple."

Belching Rewarded

The one person who never wondered about his name was Anne. She thought he had fallen straight from heaven, name and all. For one thing, he could run faster and belch louder than anyone else in the third grade. The trouble with Anne was that she was a girl; she wore blue ribbons in her golden hair, and her eyes were blue as the sky. That made her yucky, which was the reason Leaf didn't take much notice of her, even though she lived next door.

Then one day he discovered Anne sitting in a tree trying to make airplane noises. By the time Leaf had demonstrated all his best motor sounds and crashes for her, he decided Anne wasn't so yucky after all. The elderly aunt who was raising her could teach her only so much, but after a few months of help from Leaf, she had some new skills. She could even throw a great fastball, and she wasn't afraid to skin her knees.

The next twelve years passed quickly. Leaf was about to

graduate from the University and move away. He had come to spend his last Christmas vacation at home with his parents. When he walked up to the house, he wondered if that could be Anne he saw coming out of her front door. When had she turned so pretty? If she should stop near him, what could he possibly think of to say?

She smiled up at him with a pleasant hello. He watched a halo of snowflakes gather around her and catch on her pale eyelashes. He didn't feel like saying anything at all. He didn't feel like belching either.

Anne looked at him curiously. He was tall and strong now, but he had the same serious gray eyes. There was an awkward silence. Slowly, she put on her left glove, preparing to walk away. He was wishing she had a few more hands that needed gloves on them. He had to think of something fast, or soon she would be gone, and he would never see her again. Leaf cleared his throat.

His face became quite red. He heard himself ask if she might want to get married.

"It would depend on who asked me," she smiled.

"Oh…yes. Yes, that's true…" he said, looking down at his shoes. His eyes became even more serious.

Anne briefly joined him in inspecting his shoes, on the chance they deserved further attention.

"And who do you suppose might ask?" Anne wondered aloud. Watching his face closely, she began to pull on her other glove.

He blinked. "Well…there's me," he answered.

The joy crept across her face. But Leaf could hardly breathe until he was sure of it. Suddenly they found themselves laughing so hard they fell over in the snow, and Anne quite forgot where she had been going. They both forgot to feel cold until they had made snow angels all over the front yard and labeled them, "Leaf and Anne Locke, and children."

At the Bunkhouse

Zack had been glad to arrive at the bunkhouse where he would see Dan and Leaf again. Although he was several years younger than the other two, Zack was just as broad and muscular. Over the past summers, the three men had developed a trust in one another that eased them through the dangers they faced.

Zack could hardly wait to show them his new lightweight Bullard Aluminum Hardhat. It promised to protect the wearer against falling limbs, which were called "widow-makers." Because they were hot and uncomfortable, hardhats were not required, and few firefighters wore them.

Even though Zack had never known a father or brother, he felt as though he belonged to a family when he heard Leaf and Dan each speak of a wife and home. With his easy smile, the two other men found Zack's friendship natural and comfortable. He could make the two of them laugh just by making jokes about the rocks in their boots or the sand in their rations. And there was no end to the creativity of his practical jokes; no one ever figured out how the rowboat got on the roof of the Ranger Station.

Sometimes when they had a free Saturday, they would bounce along in back of the open truck to pick up the mail in town. Leaf would play his harmonica while Zack strummed his homemade guitar, bellowing all the verses of his endless supply of songs. They called these rides "cultural events," and they were the highlight of the week.

Leaf eagerly awaited the birth of his first child, and for weeks he had been expecting the important announcement from Anne. Due to the unpredictable behavior of the yet unseen baby, Anne's doctor had suggested that she stay either at the hospital or with Leaf's sister Freydis, who was twenty years older than Leaf. Freydis had been named for a sister of Leif Eriksson. Later in life, people called her Flora sometimes as well.

Though Anne would miss Leaf, she had agreed it was important for him to take part in fighting the wildfires, and she faithfully sent him entertaining letters and news clippings. Anne wrote Leaf once while she was staying with Freydis and thereafter from the hospital. However, communicating with her husband, whether by mail or by telephone, could be complicated. Aside from knowing he would be at least an eight-hour drive away, it was hard to predict where the men might be found at any given time. Even when they were within reach of the telephone, much of the time the operator couldn't put a call through, no matter how often the phone was cranked.

Occasionally either Dan or Leaf received homemade cookies or candy from home. They always shared them with Zack while sitting on the bunkhouse cots or warming their feet before the iron woodstove. One night a box came for Leaf. He found an envelope with something lumpy in it hiding under the saltwater taffy. On the front was a small hand-drawn heart under which was written, "To my Leaf. I hope it will bring good luck. Love, Anne." He looked inside and smiled, closed it, and slipped it into his pocket.

The Forest Fire

One night, after many long days of fighting fires in high winds, the three men and the other members of the crew finally had the flames contained. The air was still and drizzly. Only the occasional lightning flash illuminated a distant cloud. Now they were facing the tedious period of "mop-up." All night they would have to patrol the hill, combing it for the many hot spots that were smoldering under the surface ready to flare up at the slightest breeze. One by one, whenever the foreman could spare them, they would burrow into the warm ashes for a brief rest to gather strength for their next efforts.

That was the night Zack began inventing baby names for Leaf's amusement. "What if it's twins? They could be Pick and Pad Locke," he laughed. "Or maybe Twig and Rosebud, if you want to stick with an outdoor theme," he said. "You could always combine your names."

Kicking a root of the pine tree that towered overhead, Zack turned the axe side of his Pulaski upward, and used the hoe side to break open the tangle of roots beneath his boots. It was smoldering under the soil.

"Hey, you told us about Leif Eriksson's wife. What was her name, again?"

"Thorgunna," Leaf grinned.

"Wow! Now there's a mouthful," said Zack, wrinkling his sunburned nose. He shoveled dirt on the root to smother the embers while his mouth worked on combining "Leaf" and "Thorgunna."

Zack was about to declare all results unworthy of Leaf's amazing child, when out of nowhere came at once a deafening crack of thunder and brilliant forks of lightning. The bolt dashed the Pulaski from Dan's hands, sending the sharp blade

The Pulaski

into his thigh. The force of it hurled him unconscious onto the slope, his body lunging against Leaf.

Although his arm was badly burned, Leaf regained his breath and quickly dragged Dan out of danger. While lightning cracked and struck all around them, Leaf struggled to revive his friend. The sweat glistened on his back as embers and burning branches hissed and crashed on all sides. "Breathe, Dan. Breathe!" he cried, as he worked over Dan's motionless form.

In the confusion of darkness and blinding flashes, a limp body tumbled unnoticed down the steep bank and out of sight.

An angry gust of wind whipped across the rise, and the great tree above them exploded with a new burst of infernal heat. The foreman and other crew members rushed to assess the situation and account for all the men.

"There's no use," they agreed. "Dan's already dead. Get yourself to safety, and do it now!"

But Leaf continued stubbornly. Press and release, one… two…. Press and release, one…two…. He struggled in the heat of the roaring flames, until at long last Dan stirred, his chest rising and falling without help. He was going to live.

They were too late to save Zack. The lightning had been drawn to the metal of his hard hat; the very thing he had worn for protection caused his death. Zack's body was found crumpled at the base of the hill with his pale blue eyes open, lifeless hands gripping the handle of his Pulaski.

Gratitude

Dora felt she knew Leaf, if only through her husband's letters. As Dan was recovering from the wound in his thigh, he had written her to say that more and more there was reason to worry about Leaf. Since the death of their young friend Zack, Leaf had become very quiet and seemed to blame himself. Although nothing would make up for the loss of Zack, Dan and Dora hoped kindness toward Leaf might lighten the grief that burdened him.

Dora could think of no adequate way to thank Leaf for having saved her husband's life, but she could at least get to know Leaf's wife. It would be good to thank Anne face to face for Leaf's courage in saving Dan. Showing an interest in Anne's health might be the most comforting thing she could do for Leaf Locke.

Dora took the long train ride to Anne's hometown. As she looked out the window at the parade of cities and cornfields, she pushed back some wandering strands of hair with her delicate fingers. Dora resolved to make Anne Locke's hospital stay as pleasant as she could.

Bedside Friends

The lights had to be kept low in the hospital room to keep Anne's eyes comfortable. Still, a cheerful feeling surrounded Anne and Dora. From the time they first met, they felt as if they had been friends for years. The two women had many interests in common, and shared concern about the work their husbands were doing.

Dora wondered if Anne should ask Leaf to come home for the baby's arrival; however, she understood Anne's reluctance to call her husband away from fighting fires. The papers were full of dreadful news about how destructive the fires were this year. This was a critical time for the nation's forests, and Anne insisted she and the baby were going to be all right.

Leaf's sister, Freydis, often visited Anne at the hospital. Freydis was an English teacher who lived alone in a small bungalow. Whenever she came, she brought books from her personal library and fragrant flowers from her garden.

"Do you remember the neighbors' flowers across the street?" Anne asked Freydis.

"I do," she answered. "We never tired of seeing them from our front windows. I think their gardens were the reason Leaf chose to study botany."

"Is that why he's interested in forestry, too?" asked Dora.

"It could be," said Freydis, "although we had other neighbors down the block who spoke often of the forestlands in Norway."

Anne's cheeks appeared especially pink against the white pillowcase as she lay in the hospital bed, her yellow hair curling over the pillow.

Smiling at her sister-in-law, she said, "Freydis, tell Dora and me about Leaf when he was young."

Freydis thought a minute. "When Leaf was little, on warm summer nights we would listen to the tree frogs and chase after fireflies. Leaf never captured fireflies in a jar like most little boys do because he was sure they would miss their children.

"Did he ever tell you about Bobby, Anne?"

"Bobby who? I don't think so...."

"Bobby did his best singing about midnight," Freydis said. "Sometimes I used to awaken Leaf and carry him outside in his pajamas. We would sit and listen together on the porch swing. Leaf always sat very still to listen for fear the music would stop if he should move," she said. "Bobby had learned an amazing variety of songs in his travels. He seemed to enjoy combining them all to suit himself," she continued. "For a bird, he had a surprising sense of humor," she laughed.

"Oh!" Dora exclaimed, covering her cheeks with her small hands. She had mistakenly pictured a rather square, bearded fellow belting out something like "I've been working on the railroad...on a bicycle built for two...found a peanut, found a peanut...oh, my darling Clementine!"

"Oh, of course." Anne brightened. "I remember that mockingbird! He spent a lot of time in your cherry tree."

Freydis continued thinking about her younger brother. "Leaf always had a good ear for sound effects," she said. "I think that's why he loved the violin so early. You can understand why I was homesick for him when I went away to teach school," said Freydis.

"Leaf would put raisins just inside the kitchen window then open it," she recalled. "For several years he had Bobby hopping into the kitchen to get one raisin at a time from the windowsill. He wrote to tell me about making up his own bird songs for calling Bobby."

"He was a good teacher too," said Anne. Anne Locke was remembering an absolutely perfect day long ago when Leaf had sat with her in the tree sharing his entire repertoire of male sound effects. She asked, "Would you like to hear an owl? Maybe a car starting?"

"You could do an owl starting a car," laughed Freydis, as Anne raised her eyes to the ceiling and cleared her throat.

That evening, Anne's doctor said to his wife, "A funny thing happened today. I was in the hall outside a patient's room. It sounded like there were cars screeching and crashing in there. I didn't go in to see her, because I could tell she had visitors. Sometimes there was an orangutan or a donkey...and you should have heard them as loons doing mating calls! The three of them were having a grand time in there.

"I heard the kind of laughter that helps people get well. I hope it does. This patient has pre-eclampsia, so she's going to need it."

The Letter

Leaf asked himself repeatedly whether he could have saved Zack. Such troubling thoughts disturbed his sleep at night. His eyes stared at nothing, while his head rang with the roar of fire and the crash of thunder. However, days were busy for Leaf, and he tried to think ahead toward the news of the baby that would be coming soon.

One evening during mail call, all eyes were on a promising-looking envelope that came for Leaf. Many hands passed it to him. Surely this would be the exciting news for which he had been waiting! His hands shook as he opened the letter. Would it be a boy or a girl?

Leaf read the letter. He went over it again, hoping he had just misunderstood it the first time. Then he closed his eyes in disbelief. His lips repeated the words he had read. It began, "We regret to inform you..."

Leaf's wife had lived only long enough to name the baby. When he closed his eyes, he imagined not only the blood of his friend, but also the screams of his wife.

The next morning, without notice, quietly and suddenly, Leaf was gone. He had been taken somewhere for a long rest and treatment, with the hope that he could recover from his grief.

The only reminder of Leaf was a thick folder left on Dan's cot. Leaf had labeled it "For Daniel Lawrence." Inside were assorted papers and letters. In the bottom of the folder was a small lumpy envelope decorated with a hand-drawn heart. Turning it over, Dan realized that he had seen it before. Leaf had received it from his wife before her death, and had kept it in his pocket. It bore the words, "To my Leaf. I hope this will bring you good luck, Love, Anne."

CHAPTER SIX

You-Know-What

Melinda had waited until after study hall, when she could see Hetty alone. She took her by the arm and said, "I have a secret, and you can't tell anyone...not ever." She looked around. "Mrs. Larabee was over at our house, and I heard her tell my mom that Louisa doesn't know she's adopted."

Melinda had said, "adopted" in a low voice, like maybe if the police heard, they would take Louisa far away to some place like a concentration camp, or to a desert island with cannibals, or at least somewhere she couldn't infect nice people. Hetty thought about how dogs are taken to a pound. It always sounded like a place where they would pound the dogs to get rid of them, sort of like the way cars get squashed when you don't want them any more. Her eyes widened and she looked around the room for Louisa. Maybe Louisa would need people to be extra specially nice to her now, in case she ever found out she was "you-know-what."

That night, Hetty was holding a dresser drawer for Papa while he sanded it. "Melinda knows someone who was adopted," she said. He kept right on sanding. Hetty knew Papa wouldn't ask who it was. He always knew when to leave it be, and that's why it was always safe to say things to him. When she talked with Papa, it was a little like when they went sailing together. He let Hetty set the sails; then no matter which way she pointed the boat, the wind seemed to keep blowing. Although when he changed directions, they could end up somewhere better.

"Lots of people feel like a house is not a home without a child," he said. "Just imagine if you weren't here helping me while I sand this drawer." He whistled between his teeth for emphasis.

"It would be wonderful if all children could be raised by two parents who love them," he continued.

"Can you brace this end a little tighter against the vice, Hetty?"

Papa blew the sawdust out of a corner. "Years ago, people were made to feel ashamed of being adopted. How sad. It's very hard for couples who wait for children to come, and they never do."

He handed Hetty a worn candle to rub over the bare wood while he cleaned the workbench. "So many people benefit when there is an adoption. And there are so many people to thank.

"Often there are reasons a child isn't told about being adopted. Parents can only hope to be wise about how and when to explain it." He smiled, then brushed the sawdust from her shoulder, leaving even more of it on her sleeve.

Hetty thought, "I wonder how I would feel if I was

adopted. I'm glad I don't have to think about it."

Then Papa said, "Let's raid the icebox," so they ran up from the basement. As their two spoons scraped the last of the lemon custard out of the carton, Papa got the floor a bit sticky. Hetty noticed Mother was good at pretending not to see.

Lying in bed that night, Hetty felt certain Louisa wouldn't feel ashamed if she concentrated on being thankful. She imagined they were sitting together on Hannah's broadest branch, where it would be much easier to talk.

"Just lean back against the trunk, Louisa. You won't fall. Oh, my! Your eyes look red. What's the matter?"

"Nothing, I guess. Well, actually I just found out I'm...I mean I was..." Louisa began to sob, "adopted," she squeaked hoarsely.

"That just makes you extra special, Louisa. You have more to be thankful for than the rest of us." She hugged Louisa and used her handkerchief to wipe away her friend's tears.

"Oh, Hetty! You're always so kind. That's why everyone loves you so much." Louisa sniffed tragically. She added, "Nobody will ever talk to me again when they find out."

"I will, Louisa," replied Hetty, spreading her skirt gracefully across the branch. "Actually, I'll tell you how it is: Once upon a time your parents were positively heartbroken. That was before they adopted you. Then by absolute magic they got you, but that was only because there was somebody who really and truly loved you from the beginning... and I mean more than you can ever imagine, but they knew if you stayed with them, you'd have to live in abject poverty, and they thought you were much too special to stand in the snow without shoes hold-

ing a little tin cup with dents and begging for money so you could buy oatmeal with it. I just looked up "abject" yesterday, and it means extremely bad and miserable.

"Anyway, they wished you could live like a true princess, and at least have a mother and father who know you are absolutely and positively a dream come true, and would give you the moon if they could. At this very moment they are probably somewhere trying to imagine you sipping hot chocolate from a teacup painted with tiny flowers."

"Do you really think I'm special, Hetty?"

"Actually, everyone's going to wish they were adopted like you. Take this leaf, so you can always remember that."

Hetty started thinking how nice it would be if Mother and Papa were to adopt a brother for her. She didn't have a baby in mind. If she were to make the request, it would be for a fully-grown one; someone who did interesting things and could be good company, like Morgan was to Melinda. Morgan took Melinda with him lots of places. When he took her to his school fair, he let her invite Hetty to come, too.

One of the best things they had was a booth where people were signing up for a tire-changing demonstration. Papa had already had two flat tires in the Studebaker. Hetty could see how useful the instruction could be if she were alone with her mother when it happened. So she waited in that line while Melinda went over to the bake sale looking for pink cupcakes.

Hetty was picturing herself heroically rescuing her mother. Maybe her tire would have been punctured from running over a barbecue grate that had fallen off a garbage truck. Without help from Hetty, she would probably be without water for days and perish in the desert, or be set upon by thieves who would cut off her long braid and sell it to an Arabian princess who was hoping to be just as pretty as that when she got to be her age. But she never would be, Hetty was sure of that.

When Hetty got to the front of the line, the man in charge seemed to notice her for the first time. He said, "Oh, you're a girl," and reached around her, handing the pen to the boy in line behind her. Hetty could not argue with that, but she was disappointed it had cost her a place in line.

She would always remember what happened next. Morgan came to her defense. He marched right up to the man in charge and said, "She most certainly is not!"

Later, Hetty proudly announced to her parents that because of Morgan's kindness she could change a tire.

That night she unlaced Papa's boots from her ankles and looked at them differently. Hetty still thought of them as old friends she would never outgrow, but maybe there were times they could wait for her in the closet.

Nature Happens

The days became longer, and Olive Witch Forest stayed pleasantly light into the afternoon. Hetty had been looking in on the little ovenbird family every day. The young had hatched just two days earlier, and the mother and father came and went very stealthily, so no enemy raider would discover their young.

The parents looked so exactly like each other that Hetty wondered how they could even tell themselves apart.

Hetty still thought of them as old friends
she would never outgrow.

They must have to ask each other, "Is it my turn to tend the babies, Sweetheart, or am I the one who just did it?" The other might not know either.

"I'll babysit for a while, Dear, then if I can tell which one of us just did it, I will let you know who's who."

"Thank you."

"Oh, were you thanking me or you?"

"I'm not sure."

Actually, Hetty thought it wouldn't make much difference, they were both such nice parents.

Hetty also made friends with a busy chipmunk, watching as he climbed the stiff grasses to gather the seeds at the top. Once there, his body weight flopped the blades of grass to the ground. He did this for a very long time. Climb and flop, climb and flop. This business of gathering food was a lot of exercise!

When Hetty had stayed still for a long while, courage and curiosity brought the little striped creature ever closer to her. She could see his whiskers twitching. His eyes were alert, watching with interest how this human girl-child did her breathing and blinking.

Hetty recognized a dark brown dog with one yellow eye and one brown one. With the approach of such a large dog, the chipmunk scampered under the ferns and soon returned to gathering food.

"Hi, Gunn," Hetty said. "Nice boy." But Gunn was too busy sniffing through the low umbrellas of the May apples to be bothered with wagging his long tail. Hetty wished Pinky hadn't grown old and died. Pinky had been much friendlier than Gunn.

Hetty supposed she should go home. If she did her homework before Mother and Papa got home, they could listen to
the Jack Benny Radio Show. Back at home, she had deliberately hidden two of her after-school cookies from herself.
She sat thinking about her plan.

*Here's what I'll do: First I'll pick up my assignment book,
and I'll cover my eyes so I can't see the two things I've hidden
under it. Then I'll feel my way along the wall to get a pencil
from the jiggety-drawer, so there is absolutely no chance of those
two things I'm not thinking about ever distracting me from math
homework. Then, when I've finished absolutely every last problem, I can go back and eat the cookies as a reward.*

*Actually, maybe it would be easier to work if I'm free of any
temptations, so I guess I should get rid of the temptation right at
the start. Yes, that's the thing to do. I'd better eat both cookies
first thing when I get home.*

Hetty was still thinking when one of the ovenbirds made
a call of alarm. The other one appeared to have a broken
wing and was flapping around just a short distance from its
nest. She soon realized it was risking its own life with a broken wing act, hoping to draw attention away from its fledg-
lings in the nest. Looking toward the nest, Hetty saw the
reason for their alarm. The hungry chipmunk was running
away with two helpless baby birds in his mouth.

Hetty didn't feel like doing her math when she got home.
She didn't feel much like eating her cookies, either.

Frouncey

Guess what, Hannah. The doctor says my heart is still perfect! I had to miss school two days to go get it checked. He said the only reason I can look forward to turning fourteen next month is because I was born at the right time. They haven't known how to fix hearts like mine for very long.

We had the funnest Scrabble game ever, last night! We used to play Scrabble all the time when I had to stay home from school so much.

We decided if Shakespeare could make up lots of words, why couldn't we do it too? If it wasn't for him, we wouldn't even have gloomy or majestic! So Mother put down frouncey, then I made nostrich, and Mother made up skrunkle, for lots of points. I've forgotten the ones we invented with "Q" and "X."

We had to make up a definition at the same time and then vote on whether to accept the word. When we stopped to make some popcorn, we got absolutely snorfy and frupply from laughing, and then we started playing again. My very best one was Quatch, which is the last name of Bigfoot. I said his first name is Sas. Mother voted "no," because proper names aren't allowed. I said it wasn't really a PROPER proper name, and she was laughing so hard I couldn't tell what she was trying to say.

I told them about Melinda's uncle who has the world's biggest feet that she's never seen. I mean her uncle, not his feet. She hasn't seen him because he has shell shock and he won't ever, ever get over it and come home, she doesn't think. I told Melinda I got over my heart defect, so maybe he'll get better, too.

I asked Papa what shell shock was. He said in wars, when bombs are exploding all around and soldiers are dying, it can be really, really too hard for some people to deal with. It's like they get wounds nobody else can see. Sometimes love can help them, though. Papa's not too crazy about words like "never" and "hopeless."

CHAPTER SEVEN

Not Invited

One Monday morning a lot of excited chatter filled the hall when the girls saw each other at school.

"Color television? Really?" Laura was doubtful.

"Yes! Can you believe it?" Melinda exclaimed.

"But how do they get the color in there?"

Hetty couldn't imagine how Hop Along Cassidy or Howdy Doody might look with the added confusion of color. When she and her parents had seen them once, the screen was all splotched with white and had zigzaggy stripes. They hadn't been sure television would amount to much, so for now they would just be satisfied with the radio.

But this was different.

"Gretchen's father is a really, really important person who has something to do with RCA," Melinda explained, "and he's put a television in the hotel, specially to show us for her birthday party!"

Hetty waited to see how she figured into the plan.

Five days later, Hetty got a glimpse here and there of brightly wrapped birthday presents peeking out from the students' desks or pockets.

Hetty felt sick to her stomach. She didn't have a birthday present for Gretchen. Was there something about this she was supposed to know?

At the end of the school day, Gretchen's mother waited in the hall for class to be dismissed. Hetty could hear her. "The cars are all waiting to take you straight to the hotel. Be sure to have your invitations with you, girls, because that will be your ticket to get in." She spoke in a loud and musical voice.

Hetty was puzzled. "Invitation?" She felt the heat creeping into her cheeks. "I don't know anything about an invitation."

There was a blur of books, gifts, and the precious invitations. No one noticed Hetty in the rush and confusion. She stayed in her seat, blinking so the tears wouldn't show.

Her mind raced:

Maybe Gretchen was embarrassed to invite me. Or maybe her mother had said, "You can have a party, but only on the condition that you won't invite that Lawrence girl. I don't like her looks, and I hear she never opens her mouth and she's different, and she stirs her ice cream."

The halls became quiet. Miss Hacket looked in as she walked past the classroom door. Almost immediately, she returned and was standing next to Hetty's desk.

"You're not going to the party, Hetty?" She sounded surprised. Hetty shook her head.

Gretchen's mother must not have told Miss Hacket how she doesn't want Gretchen to have me for a friend.

"I can drive you to the hotel if you've missed your ride." Miss Hacket was speaking softly.

Hetty looked down at her desk. She traced her finger over the words someone had scratched into the surface years ago. It was the school motto, "*Inveniam viam aut faciam.*" She would have to think about that. "*I will find a way or make one.*" She wondered whether the motto contained any special message for her at this moment.

Hetty would be ashamed to tell Mother and Papa that she hadn't been invited to the party. She thought she would feel better if she could go to Hannah.

"Is everything all right, Hetty?" asked Miss Hacket.

Hetty nodded, and said, "Well, I…umm…." She felt for her handkerchief.

Miss Hacket sat down next to her, squeezing herself into Melinda's desk.

She looked into Hetty's eyes and said, "I don't want anything to be making you unhappy. Is there some reason you couldn't go to the party?"

"I…well, I have to go home," Hetty said in a whisper.

She looked over at Miss Hacket.

"She probably looked like Snow White before she got wrinkly," thought Hetty, "except she doesn't have a red bow in her hair."

Miss Hacket placed her hand warmly on Hetty's. Her face was kind and sympathetic. Hetty imagined the words Miss Hacket might be thinking:

If it were my birthday party, you would be sitting next to me and I would give you the cherry off the top of my hot fudge sundae, and you and Bashful, and Doc, and Dopey, and Grumpy, and Sleepy, and Sneezy, and Happy would be the only people I would need to invite, unless I've forgotten any of their names. You could blow out my candles and keep the wish for yourself.

To Like or Not to Like

That evening, when supper was over, Mother poured hot Ovaltine into three mugs. Hetty had been waiting for the right time to ask a question.

"I was just wondering about a bunch of things. Like for instance, what would you do if somebody doesn't like you?"

Papa didn't say anything at all.

"It's just a for instance," Hetty added, wondering if she sounded nonchalant enough. She thought:

I hope I sound kind of casual, like if I was just floating along on a raft, and then I happened to notice a bottle with an anonymous note in it floating next to the raft, and when I casually opened it, the note just happened to say, "To whoever reads this, I don't like you very much. Sincerely, your friend, Anonymous."

"You seem to think I would do something." Papa stated.

"I mean, should I decide to not like them back?"

"What would that accomplish, Hetty?"

There wasn't an answer that sounded very nice.

"Whether or not people like you is their problem," Papa said. Hetty doubted anybody would think Gretchen had any problem. "If there's anything to be done, work on the way you feel about them, instead."

Hetty considered the school motto: I will find a way or make one. "Maybe that means I ought to find a way to like her," Hetty said, "...that is, if it was me."

"Good thinking, Hetty," Papa said casually, honking his nose.

Hetty thought some more:

It's like we're all on the raft together, and we just happen to see another bottle with a note, so we pull out the cork, and the note says, "Ha, ha, April Fools," and that means we don't have to worry about the first note anymore.

"Think how complicated it would be to hate people," Papa continued, spilling Ovaltine on the table. "and what a waste of a possible friendship."

Mother floated a marshmallow in each mug. "A smile can go a long way, Hetty," she said, "and some people could use a smile more than you think."

No Hard Feelings

In addition to having their desks next to each other, Melinda and Hetty had been assigned adjacent gym lockers. Gretchen always changed for gym near them, probably because their lockers had been assigned alphabetically. Hetty thought there might be other ways of assigning seats and lockers. She thought:

If I were the teacher, I know what I would do. In gym class, the girls could be divided up by blood type, in case there were any accidents, and they needed to give each other transfusions.

And then maybe at lunchtime everyone could be divided up according to how healthy they were. Depending if you won or lost at arm wrestling, you'd sit at different tables.

There could be a sign over the unhealthy table saying something like "Dream Girls," everyone would want to be a dream girl, so they would sit down all excited about turning into Miss America or something, so they'd get fish and broccoli, and when it was time for dessert, the servers would say, "Oh my, we seem to be fresh out of hot fudge sundaes with sugar wafers and little pink sprinkles in the whipped cream, but you could have a scoop of air, with a sauce of delicately scented pink water."

And it's not like the sign would be lying or anything like that, because they really would be dreaming. Mostly about food they didn't get.

Before Hetty had started working out a menu for the healthy table, Gretchen stopped next to her. With a look of sudden puzzlement, she asked Hetty, "How come you didn't come to my party?"

"I...well... um...," Hetty blushed. She couldn't think of a good answer that wouldn't sound like an accusation. She didn't have to. Melinda jumped right in and said to Gretchen, "You got your buttons in the wrong buttonholes!"

Hetty looked directly at Gretchen and smiled. Gretchen looked like she could use a smile. At that moment, Hetty decided things were looking better, and it wasn't just the buttons. She was glad it had just been by mistake that Gretchen hadn't invited her.

After Gretchen left, Melinda gave a summary of the

birthday party. "There was this clown that gave us cotton candy, and then we saw the television, and it was really boring!" She slumped her shoulders as if she were ready to start snoring right now, in a standing position. Melinda looked as bored as possible, by sighing and rolling her eyes in a cross-eyed sort of way. Hetty thought it must be extremely hard to entertain Melinda. Her mind wandered:

Melinda says her parents actually had a circus elephant come to her house once. So if the Queen of England came for tea she probably wouldn't think it was very interesting. Not even if Her Majesty did something like put her hands in a Howdy Doody puppet and made it tell jokes.

Suddenly Hetty realized what Melinda had been doing, and why she had used her most popular and convincing boredom act. She had done it so Hetty wouldn't find out how tragic it was that she had missed the party.

CHAPTER EIGHT

The Winner

Morgan had driven over to Haxton after school to pick up his sister. He approached a group of girls he judged to be Hetty's age. "Excuse me. Do you know where I might find Hetty Lawrence?"

The girls were so startled at seeing a boy on the school grounds, and especially one so worth noticing, that they giggled inaudible answers and gawked at him as he thanked them and returned to his car.

At last Melinda and Hetty emerged from the school at the same time. "Let me carry some of those," he said, glancing at their stacks of books.

Hetty knew he was strong enough to carry a ton of stuff, but she didn't want to be any trouble. "That's okay," she said, "I'll keep them here till the bus drives up."

"I wanted to find you," said Morgan, "to thank you for the advice. I got my crystal set working. Now I can listen to

'*The Great Gildersleeve*!'" He followed with a lively imitation of Gildy's inane laugh.

"Can you do Baby Snooks, too?" asked Hetty. He answered by talking like Donald Duck instead. Hetty laughed so hard she had to sit down on the steps to keep from falling over.

As soon as Morgan and Melinda drove away, she realized the buses had departed without her while she had been talking with Morgan. It was such a long way to walk home that she wasn't sure what to do, but she went to the assembly hall where the students waited for the buses when they went on field trips. Hetty thought somehow if she waited long enough, a bus might magically appear. She had hoped so, with all the intensity she could muster.

She had almost concluded that wishing for something wasn't enough to make it happen when a bus pulled up outside the window. It was a small Bluebird bus. She watched students come from the open doors and thought of circus clowns she had seen come out of a Volkswagen. Hetty didn't think Bluebird was a very suitable name for a bus. Having recently read *Moby-Dick,* she thought buses might be named for a whale instead. Something like Moby Bus.

The students came into the assembly hall and formed a line before a long table. Several men and women materialized and were handing out large numbers to hang from the necks of the waiting students.

One woman walked briskly from across the room and led Hetty to the line, saying, "Here's where you're supposed to be."

Hetty was inclined to cooperate with official-looking people, and the woman had looked particularly official, judging by the number of dog-eared pages on her clipboard and the harried look on her face. She planted Hetty behind a tall girl with small glasses and a short boy with big ones. They were among the few people who seemed to know each other.

There was only one person Hetty knew, but she didn't recognize Hetty back. It was Izzy, the smartest girl at Haxton Academy. Izzy was wearing a large number 14 over her Haxton uniform.

The lady who was handing out numbers looked at Hetty. "Name of sponsor?" she asked.

Before Hetty had time to explain she was really only there looking for a ride home, there was a sudden commotion, and some papers dropped behind the table. The numbers lady lost track of what she had been doing, until the harried official lady breezed over to help her reorganize her thoughts.

"That's Nelly. Give her the eleven," she said, moving on to solve the next problem.

Hetty had heard many variations of her name. She had usually answered to anything close to it, including Nelly. Well, maybe not Henny. She had nothing personal against chickens, but that was almost her least favorite name. Only Henny Penny could be worse.

Then as Hetty watched and listened from the far corner of the hall, something exciting happened. Students in various shapes and sizes were given words to spell. They stood in rows on the stage, and were assigned really and truly wonderful words, some of which were Hetty's old friends. Others were new discoveries that she wrote down, hoping to make them hers forever.

"Number 5," said a man with a microphone, "spell *superannuation.*"

Number 5 shifted his weight a few times and closed his eyes.

"Superannuation," he repeated.

Hetty wondered if Number 5 was trying to remake some wishes he'd used up in the past, or to collect one he hadn't made after he'd broken a wishbone. The crowd sighed as he missed the word.

It was all so much fun for Hetty that she completely forgot she needed to find a way to get home. Nor did she protest when a faceless adult found her and guided her to the stage.

She listened to more amazing words coming from the microphone. The man with the microphone had a very clear voice, almost like Papa's. The spotlights were pleasantly warm. She thought it was a little like sitting in Hannah's branches having the sun shining on her, and it helped that the lights obscured the faces of the people in the audience.

"Number 11," said the nice voice, "spell *nidulation.*"

Since *"nid"* was French for "nest," Hetty guessed this must be another way of saying, "nest making." This was too fun to believe! The word was just meant for her. She would spell it in memory of the baby ovenbirds. Hetty repeated the word, and began to spell it out.

"Speak up, honey," said a voice behind her, "so the judges can hear you."

Hetty spoke right up, just like when the family used to play word games on summer car trips. They had to yell to be heard over the noisy air cooler hanging in the opening of the front window. They had laughed about the obsolete word *aquabob,* an outdated way to say *icicle.* Hetty had said how much quieter it would have been to dangle aquabobs in the window to cool the car.

Hetty got that word right. And the next, and the next. Hetty hesitated at the word *slubbergedullion,* but she got that one right, too. Number 24 missed *tziganologist,* but Hetty knew that one. It was the word for a person who studies Hungarian gypsies.

Hetty knew the word because she had read quite a lot about gypsies. In a brief but frightening encounter, her Grandmother Jenny had been stolen by gypsies when she was a baby. Little Jenny's frantic mother had the wits to run after the thieves and remove the baby's bonnet and shoes, which she offered instead. Hetty often wondered how different her own upbringing might have been if the gypsies had insisted on keeping her grandmother Jenny instead of the baby clothes.

The voice hurled the words at Hetty more rapidly now. There was *confabulate,* then *plenipotentiary.*

As her eyes became accustomed to the lights, Hetty saw Mrs. Fairburn applauding from the back. After Hetty spelled *doggerel,* she saw the headmistress rush out the door. When Mrs. Fairburn returned with whatever Haxton Academy people she could collect from the halls, they all stood together cheering and clapping for Izzy and Hetty. Izzy was soon eliminated by the word *yclept,* a word Hetty wouldn't have known either.

Miss Altoona contributed the most noise during the applause. She was smiling, and although she had her little book with her, she wasn't putting any red pencil marks in it. When the contest was over, Hetty was the only one left standing. The applause continued a while even after the announcer had asked the audience to please be quiet.

He said, "The winner is number 11. Congratulations,

young lady! A very impressive accomplishment." He looked
out at the audience and all around the edges of the hall. "Will
the photographer please come to the front? Do Mr. and Mrs.
Adams happen to be here?

"Miss Adams, would you come down off the stage? We
have an award to present to you."

"Miss Adams," said another nice voice that became louder
and more insistent.

The nice voice repeated the request several more times.
People were looking directly at Hetty, but calling for a Miss
Adams at the same time. She stood on the stage, awaiting fur-
ther instructions.

Hetty watched Mrs. Fairburn run over to the judges' table. The announcer covered his microphone to muffle their
animated conversation. After a long five minutes, her headmistress ran up the steps toward her on the stage.

Mrs. Fairburn gave Hetty a warm enthusiastic hug. "Congratulations, Champion," she said in her ear. Putting her arm
around Hetty's waist, she turned to the stage microphone and
added, "We have been privileged to see an amazing performance this afternoon. Thank you to all the many people who
have been responsible for such a success. It has been a pleasure to host this first contest here at Haxton Academy, and we
look forward to many more such events."

There was more loud clapping, after which Mrs. Fairburn
said, "We will now hear from the chairman, Mr. Langley."

With little mincing steps, Mr. Langley gradually inched
his way to the stage spotlights, as if he needed time to think.

There was a long mysterious pause, until he brightened
and said, "Our lovely *cymotrichous* contestant has set a high
standard for the future."

There was general laughter as the audience recalled it was the word meaning *wavy-haired* that someone had spelled correctly. He seemed relieved when more laughter followed. It allowed him time to keep groping for how to explain what had happened.

"It seems there has been an irregularity," he continued. "An irregularity is just what there has been; irregular is all it was. It seems the young lady who has won was not properly registered or pre-qualified. We cannot award the trophy to her for that reason."

Hetty felt the heat creeping into her cheeks. She felt foolish and ashamed about what she had done.

Mr. Langley shuffled his feet and looked over at Mrs. Fairburn. "However, Mrs. Fairburn, the principal of her school, has a presentation to make to the amazing Miss Henrietta Annette Lawrence."

As soon as Mrs. Fairburn mounted the stairs to the stage and smiled at Mr. Langley with her soft gray eyes, everything seemed just as it should be.

She gathered Hetty into the spotlight and said, "Thank you for being a credit to your school and your community, Hetty. With this number," she continued, "please know you are considered fully qualified and pre-registered for the next contest. The number you wore this afternoon is yours to keep."

Mrs. Fairburn left the spelling bee committee to sort out the awards without her help, and chose instead to drive Hetty home.

The morning paper had a short but prominently placed article:

"TOWN ABUZZ OVER QUEEN OF THE BEE."

The First Annual State Spelling Bee, hosted by the Hax-ton Academy for Girls, has found a honey of a winner. It seems Henrietta Annette Lawrence was simply "looking for a way to get home," when she unwittingly invaded the hive with no pre-vious knowledge of the contest. The number "11" the judges gave her was available only because contestant Nelly Adams had broken her leg earlier, by falling into a storm sewer.

Librarian Marian Reed, who attended the event, was not surprised by the win. Miss Reed does not know Miss Lawrence personally, but is well acquainted with her broad and eudae-monic★ reading habits.

★ Producing happiness and wellbeing; one of the spelling words in the contest.

Fall and Rescue

Hetty was surprised by the attention. It had been reward enough to have Mrs. Fairburn give her a ride home after the contest.

In math class, the first thing Miss Hacket said was, "Let's give Hetty a round of applause!" They all knew what she was talking about. "Good for you, Hetty," she added as they all cheered.

Madame du Pré whispered in her ear, *"Très bien, Mad-emoiselle!"*

Several friends had clipped the article from the paper to give her. Sue brought a copy to her at lunch. Morgan had cut out a copy for Melinda to give Hetty. He had written at the bottom, "I hope you're not too famous now to talk to normal people!" Hetty puzzled over his comment. She had always found it hard talking to people, but it wasn't because of being famous.

She wondered, "Will I have to get better at talking to people so they won't think I feel too important?"

She found Hannah, and climbed to where she could consider Morgan's message more carefully. "Maybe it doesn't matter what people think," Hetty said aloud.

Reaching the bridge she had built, she crossed over it from Hannah to her cliff cave. The spelling bee word *nidulation* came to her mind as she approached the nest she had made. She couldn't see her dictionary or the library book she had left there the previous week, as her eyes had not adjusted to the darkness of her nest.

She heard a low guttural growl ahead of her. Two eyes were glowing through the darkness. One was brown, and the other blue. It was Gunn, snarling at her with his lips curled back from his sharp white teeth.

Frightened, Hetty stepped back slowly, feeling for the bridge with the heel of her boot. Gunn leapt up at her and wrapped his front paws around her leg, snarling and snapping as he pushed his full weight against her. Hetty tried to edge closer to the bridge, but as her only hope of escape was directly behind her, she stumbled and fell, fingernails grabbing at the little ledge on her way down. She clutched the rocks in her fist until she hit the ground.

A sharp, severe pain in her shoulder made everything around her turn hollow and gray. The cliff was whirling and tumbling around her, as Hetty gasped for air, then lay still on the leaves for a time.

Whether they were words she heard or thoughts she felt, Hetty became aware of a quiet comfort reaching her through the gray hollowness of her confusion. A still voice

of perfect mildness reassured her, and two strong arms eased
under her back to lift her.

Maybe she was watching a dream play out before her,
as she drifted in and out of awareness. The dream was of
someone tall and powerful who cradled her securely, her
head resting against his chest. As he carried her past the dark
swirling emptiness, every step pounded in her head; at times
to a heartbeat, or to the rhythm of his steady breathing.

As the pain began again, snatches of Papa's poem played
in her mind.

"What is it like, Papa, going to Heaven?"

A resurgence of pain spun the darkness around her, until
the dream returned, and she felt a hand touch her cheek.

*"...He'll make you well with the power of love, and touch
your cheek, like me."*

*But Papa, you said I don't need to know about Heaven
just yet! Is that true?*

*You told me that when I was small I would hide my eyes,
and then I'd think you weren't there because I couldn't see
you. If I open my eyes now, will it change what's real? Am
I supposed to keep my eyes closed? If I open them, will I be
dead?*

Hetty felt the sun, and knew she was out of Olive Witch
Forest now. Whatever had happened? Everything seemed so
blurry.

The walking slowed; a series of doors opened and Hetty
was carried through them. The arms that had carried her

now laid her down with care. The voice of a woman joined that of her rescuer. Soon the muffled words of their continued conversation reached her from the next room. A doctor would be coming.

Hetty opened her eyes to find herself on a couch. She hadn't died. She was in a room surrounded by books. It must be the library. The door opened, and in walked a woman Hetty had seen at the spelling bee the day before.

"Hello, Annette," she smiled. "I'm Marian Reed."

The appropriate reaction to her rescuer had been beyond her ability to envision, and Hetty lacked the strength to think it through. But she didn't need to; he had left her in the care of an angel named Marian, who would stay by her side throughout the examination. Marian had freckles and a face like fresh air.

When Dr. Davidson entered the room, his broad grin seemed to arrive before the rest of him. Each smile that stretched across his face widened his large nose along with it.

"How are we doing?" he asked cheerfully. "What have we done to ourself?"

"Doctor Davidson probably says "we," to mean himself and his nose," thought Hetty. "He and his nose do work rather well together."

The doctor's cheerful nose continued to spread impressively, and she knew Mother had been right to say a smile could go a long way. It was the perfect medicine to administer while fixing her dislocated shoulder. He pulled back his sleeves and placed his hands in position. She gasped with one last hot stab of pain that expanded into her neck and across her back, then suddenly was over. There came relief she hadn't expected. Doctor Davidson had put her shoulder right; all with a grin.

Hetty heard the doctor giving a lengthy report to her rescuer, who had been waiting in the next room. After Dr. Davidson returned to say goodbye to Hetty, his partner, the smiling nose, disappeared with him from the room.

Once Hetty was alone with Marian, she thought how the library must be the very best place there was, next to Heaven. Dora had known Hetty would like Marian, but she couldn't have foreseen the way the two of them would be laughing together at the soda fountain that evening. After they had shared a chocolate milkshake, Hetty was delivered to her home with one arm in a sling, bruised but happy.

For some time, Marian Reed thought about what she had learned at the library. She thought especially about the tall man with soft gray eyes from whom she had heard it. She would keep it all to herself.

Whack-a-mole

Sometimes Leaf held imaginary conversations with Anne as he looked at her photograph. In the beginning, his sorrow had been nearly unbearable, but with the passage of time, it had become comforting to pretend she was still there talking with him. As he picked up her picture in its frame, he looked at her eyes and remembered how the snowflakes had caught in her lashes. She seemed very close in his mind.

Anne blinked and spoke directly. "Marian Reed is a nice girl," she said.

"That's just it. She's a girl. She's too young for me," he said, pausing to look out the window.

"She'll get older," Anne assured him.

"You didn't," Leaf reminded her.

"That's because I'm dead," she replied. "Our daughter An-
nette likes her," she added.

"You're the only one for me, Anne. I'm so afraid I'll forget all
the little things I loved about you. Like the way you smell. I try
very hard to hang onto those memories."

"I didn't know I smelled," she said with alarm. "How do I
smell?"

"That's exactly the problem. I can't remember," he explained.

"It doesn't matter," she reassured him. "At least you'll be
able to remember what I look like, because of Annette, or Netty, or
Hetty, or whatever people call our daughter. I guess she doesn't like
to be called Henrietta any more than I did.

"Maybe the initials on my handkerchief shouldn't have de-
cided her name," she sighed. "She could have been the heroine in
a Russian novel," Anne added, "the way they all have so many
names. It's a good thing their books all have a 'who's who' page
printed in front."

Then Anne added cheerfully, "I'm so happy we had that year
together, Leaf."

"But I was gone when you needed me," he said. "I'm so
sorry...."

"It wouldn't have turned out any differently," she said firmly.

"I wish I'd told you I love you one more time, Anne."

"You know that wasn't necessary," she smiled.

Without his saying the words, Anne had always known how
he felt. He hadn't needed to feel guilty all those years.

Anne still had something on her mind. "You might have used
the word 'fragrance,' or 'aroma.' Anything but the word 'smell,'"
she said, cocking her head the way he thought she used to do, only
he wasn't so sure anymore. He felt a bit muddled, and wondered

if maybe he was confusing it with the way Marian Reed had held her head when she looked up at him.

"You really can't think how I smelled?" Anne asked.

Leaf couldn't think how she smelled, but he took a deep breath and tried to explain the truth about why he couldn't.

"Since seeing Miss Reed at the library," he said, "I've worked especially hard to remember things like that about you. I try to picture the way you looked, but you seemed to be floating away from me. It's her face that keeps coming up instead."

He and Anne had once played Whack-a-mole at the carnival. The moles kept coming up, but the two of them had been so quick at pounding them back in their holes with their mallets that the little painted rodents didn't stand a chance. Anne had never parted with all the stuffed animals they won.

She had read his mind. "You don't need to play Whack-a-mole for my sake," she said.

Suddenly he remembered: "Cedar! That's what it was. You smelled like fresh cedar."

"Like in the bottom of a hamster cage?" Anne asked.

She straightened his tie, then squinted and spread out both her hands to cover it. It was the one with the crooked polka dots, and he vaguely remembered she used to hide it so he wouldn't wear it.

"Is it so bad that Marian's face keeps coming up?" she asked. "You're letting it happen. You mean to, because you have enough love to go around."

Just before Anne floated away, she reminded him, "I'll always be here, Leaf."

Leaf realized he was laughing out loud. It was true he was letting it happen. It was because he had absolutely no desire to whack Miss Reed on the head and make her disappear. Leaf wished he could lift Anne into the air and swing her around to show his gratitude, but he couldn't. After all, she was dead.

CHAPTER NINE

Potato Peelings

The next day, Marian's thoughts dwelt on what had happened in the library the previous afternoon. Above all she reviewed her conversation with the tall man who had been so tender with Hetty. She could still see the warmth of his gray eyes.

Marian remembered the phrase she had read in the Elizabeth Bibesco book: *To others we are not ourselves but performers in their lives cast for a part we do not even know we are playing.* Now Marian rearranged the idea to suit herself. She had seen those people just as they were, and hoped they might soon perform an important part in her life.

In elementary school, Marian had performed in a play dressed as an oversized marigold. She was supposed to remain hidden as a seed throughout the beginning of the play, then pop out of a giant flowerpot and say, "…in the sun!" at the appropriate moment. Instead, thinking no one would notice, she kept raising her head very slowly to look mournfully around at every face in the crowd. Every time she sprouted prematurely, her performance provoked an outburst of laughter from the audience. She had been looking for Joey. He was the one man her mother married who Marian loved and missed. She had hoped Joey might come back to see her.

By the time Marian got home from the library, she was thinking about how a lot of her life had been spent hiding her head in a flowerpot. Maybe now was the time to come out of hiding and play her small part well.

As she approached her home, she discovered a package leaning against the front door. Above the return address, someone had scrawled her mother's name. The handwriting was not familiar. It had been almost a year since Marian had last been able to locate her mother, and she wondered why she would be hearing from her now.

The package contained some letters addressed, "To Mistress Marian Reed." They were all personal letters. Her mother had already opened them, but had never shown them to her in all these years. The oldest of the letters had been postmarked twenty-five years ago. There were birthday cards, an Easter card, and an empty one that said," I wish I could have sent you more than this, but maybe this dollar can buy something for your Daisy Doll." Best of all, there was a cartoon of a soldier sitting on a pile of potatoes, peeling them.

All the letters to Marian were signed, "I love you, from Joey."

The last of Joey's letters he had sent to Marian from Australia shortly before his death. Marian's mother had died, and someone was now distributing her belongings.

In life, her mother had parceled out love very sparingly.

She expected others to do the same, for fear it would get all used up. Joey had known there was enough love to go around. Now in death her mother could no longer hide Joey's big heart.

That night, Marian Reed sat in her rocking chair. She rocked and thought about Joey. He had loved her after all.

Company for Lunch

Dora made a big pot of ham and potato soup and two loaves of sweet Sally Lunn bread which she cut in fat slabs and slathered with honey butter. She had called to invite Marian Reed to join them.

They sat at the sunny kitchen table as the aroma filled the house. Just before they began ladling the soup into the large earthenware bowls, Melinda's brother Morgan knocked on the kitchen door. He was reluctant to stay for lunch for fear he would be imposing, but Dora insisted that all she had to do was put another bean in the pot.

"This is possibly the best soup I've ever had," said Dan, as Dora helped him mop up the soup he had spilled down the front of his shirt.

"It's actually quite ordinary," she protested. Hetty knew better; Mother had made it mostly by improvising. It was definitely magic soup.

Marian asked Dan and Dora, "How did you meet one another?"

Since they weren't exactly sure, Dan gave his usual answer. "Our memory is that a large bird was flying off with her. I rescued her from his beak just in time."

Papa dropped some crumbs around his plate and on the

rug beneath him. Mother picked them up, and Hetty realized why a large bird might have been lurking nearby in the first place. It was waiting to see what Papa might drop.

Dan asked Marian if she had made plans for the summer.

"Nothing definite," she answered, "but I hope to be house-sitting for a friend. I was there last week, and the best part about it was taking care of their three-year-old they call Gorilla."

Amused, Dora said, "Tell us about Gorilla, Marian."

"I took her to church with me and told her I liked to listen to the sermon and maybe she would too. I had hoped to keep her occupied for a while with my new key chain that has a little brass angel on it. I got it so I can remember to see the angel in Gorilla.

"When she got restless, I was glad I'd brought along a little sack of Cheerios too," Marian continued. "I told her, 'Be really careful with them, Gorilla.'

"She pulled my hair back and breathed in my ear for a very long time until my hair was rather damp, then she finally whispered 'Okay' very sweetly in my ear.

"She was careful, all right," Marian laughed. "She found the slot in the hymn book where the spine had become separated from the back, and she poked the Cheerios in there with such care that I didn't even notice. It got everybody's attention when she closed the book. They crunched, and all the little crumbs came out the bottom onto the red carpet.

"She loves to poke things into places they don't belong," Marian explained.

Hetty could tell what Papa was thinking:

He's remembering when I was three and I found a nostril-

sized pebble. You never know for sure if something like that is going to fit unless you try. I found out that a Tinkertoy was perfect for pushing it way up my nose. But it wasn't so good for digging it out again, that's for sure. At least it's not how the doctor removed it.

While no one was watching, Papa winked at Hetty. She appreciated his tactful silence.

They listened as Marian continued.

"When the man next to me wagged his finger at Gorilla," said Marian, "she started to cry, so I had to take her out in the middle of the sermon. She screamed, 'Help me, Sermon!'

"I guess the way I'd said it, she thought 'Sermon' was the name of the man at the podium.

"Nothing she does surprises me any more.

"I know you'd love Gorilla too. When we got in the car she hugged me around the neck and tried to feed me what was left in her sack."

Hetty looked at Marian's freckled nose. She thought Gorilla was lucky to have someone like Marian caring for her.

Bronze Giants

Hetty noticed Morgan's black eye had healed, but he now had a bruise on the other cheek and jaw. When Dan drew him into the conversation, she was surprised to learn Morgan would be fighting forest fires for the summer.

"I might not have thought of it until Hetty talked about the Forest Service," said Morgan. "Someday I'd like to fly, but for now I'm interested in radio communications. Did you have a good radio system when you were there?"

Dan glanced at Dora. Neither one could suppress a

chuckle.

"Let's see. Where should I begin?" Dan wondered.

He questioned whether he should begin at all, but Dora had that twinkle in her eye that was saying, "This is the right moment to tell it; enough time has passed to reduce the humiliation."

Morgan stopped buttering his bread and listened expectantly.

"Typically," Dan began, "in the fire crew, we kept our shirts off all summer long during the day. We mainly had to wear them for fire protection.

"The men came from a variety of backgrounds. Some were there to get in shape for the football season, others were there to earn money for college. But it didn't take long for everyone to become tough and muscular. And very brown from all the sun."

Hetty could picture the jolly, shaggy-haired group, all fully aware of their extreme masculinity.

"One evening when we were all together in the bunkhouse," Dan continued, "a fellow named Rob stopped in front of the mirror and flexed his muscles. He said for everyone to hear, 'Oh, Bronze Giant, don't you ever die!'

"That's when we began laughingly calling ourselves the Bronze Giants.

"Shortly after that, when there was a lightning strike, one of the lookouts spotted a three-man fire. Leaf, Zack and I were trucked as close to the fire as possible then had to walk the rest of the way by compass. We each had a shovel and a Pulaski. The maps, food and water were in our backpacks. It was hours before we reached our destination; it was a huge yellow pine burning up on a ridge top.

"Without a two-man crosscut saw we knew it would take days to clear a safe retreat path and then to fell and limb the tree. We could see the lookout off in the distance on a mountain peak, and we tried to radio our status report through there and on to the ranger station. In this situation, normally we could have expected a truck to bring us a saw. At least as far as the road.

"We called, 'KOD75, KOD75, this is Beaver Creek fire number twelve. Come in, please!' We'd repeat that over and over.

"Meanwhile, we worked at making cuts to form a forty-five degree hinge in the directional cut line, and another cut on the opposite side, several inches higher. Only one man is supposed to chop at a time, so the second acted as a spotter, watching out for their safety, and the third would keep trying to make radio contact. When there was absolutely no response, we set the radio aside.

"But not for long. Zack thought he might as well speak into the dead radio, as if he had a live audience. He really got into it. He'd say things like, 'Ladies and gentlemen, we present to you a moment of sheer heroism, as the three Bronze Giants of the woods bring down the Massive Forest Monarch. Listen to the cry of the cambium layer as it succumbs to the rippling muscles of the Brawny Leaf Locke himself!'

"Then Leaf would do a creative imitation of how a cambium layer in distress might sound.

"I remember Zack announced to the listening audience that what they had just heard was more likely 'the mating call of the yellow-bellied whippersnapper,' or some such nonexistent bird.

"He tried again and again to reach the lookout. I still remember how it went: 'KOD75, KOD75, this is Beaver Creek fire number twelve. Come in, please!'

"We'd shift responsibilities again.

"When Leaf would open a tin of cornbread or something, or Zack tore off some jerky, I joined in to provide the narrative:

"'The Bronze Giants will now take in the nutrition necessary to sustain them as they battle the flaming monster above. We now bring you Bronze Giant Zackary Bond.'

"I was having a great time. I'd say, 'Chew for the American public, Mr. Bond!'

"And then, 'KOD75, KOD75, this is Beaver Creek fire number twelve. Come in, please!' Still no response.

"Then Leaf would get on it and maybe he'd say, 'Such heroism is unequaled in the annals of history. Daniel Lawrence strikes the blade of his Pulaski deep into the heartwood. His bulging muscles tame the previously indomitable Woodland Monarch.' He'd continued quite a while. 'Ladies and gentlemen, we pause briefly while Bronze Giant Daniel Lawrence clears his sinuses. Blow your nose for the American public.'

Hetty envisioned Papa taking out his red kerchief to produce two of his better honks.

"After days of chopping, the Mighty Bronze Giants yelled, 'Timber!' for the benefit of all our imaginary listeners.

"Leaf announced, 'Remember you heard it here, uninterrupted by commercial breaks.'

"The three of us had to remain there watching for flare-ups for another twenty-four hours after we'd seen the last of the smoke. All that time we continued the radio broadcasts.

"We walked the four hours back to the road, spent that

night in a sheep camp and got up early next morning," Dan continued. "We kept up the Bronze Giant act with all our babbling. I remember we even sang about the old gray mare that ain't what she used to be."

Morgan and Marian were both convulsed with laughter. "It's a lucky thing the radio wasn't working," Hetty said. "Just imagine if they'd heard you!"

Dan glanced at Dora and gathered the courage to continue.

"Actually, they *did*," he said.

"Oh, no!" came the gasp.

"It was three in the afternoon when we walked into the Beaver Creek Ranger Station," Dan said.

"Tell them who was there waiting for you," said Dora.

Dan leaned back in his chair and said, "As we crossed the bridge, they were all there waiting." He began to count on his fingers: "The Forest Supervisor, the Forest Dispatcher, the District Forest Ranger, the Alternate Ranger, and the Assistant Ranger.

"The first thing they said to us was, 'Well, if it isn't the bronze giants!' so we knew we were in trouble. It seems we had been jamming the radios all over the forest for days, while everyone had to put up with hearing the exploits of the Bronze Giants."

Something On His Mind

The enjoyment of one another's company continued with the bustle of shaking the crumbs off the linen tablecloth and pushing in the chairs. While Hetty washed the dishes, Morgan dried the spoons. The way Morgan kept wiping the same spoon long after he had done a thorough job of it, she thought maybe he had something on his mind. She wondered if she ought to ask about his bruises, but thought better of it.

"Thanks for being a good friend to Melinda," Morgan said finally. "I hope you won't mind keeping in touch with her while I'm gone." He kept drying the spoon. "Maybe things will be better at home while I'm gone; I think she'll be safe."

Hetty remembered Melinda had told her Morgan was the one who helped her with her homework. It was lucky Melinda wouldn't have any schoolwork to worry about until Morgan's return. Maybe Marian could help her with the summer reading list.

CHAPTER TEN

Crime Report

Hetty went to Hannah to finish reading *Pride and Prejudice*, but her mind wandered to thoughts that had been weighing on her.

What have I done, Hannah? I don't understand what happened at the spelling bee. Maybe I ruined it and nobody's telling me. Somebody should have told me I'm not Nelly Adams. Actually, I knew I wasn't but I hope nobody thought I was pretending like I was. Maybe not speaking up is the same as pretending, and pretending is the same as lying?

Maybe Nelly would have won bigger than I did if she hadn't fallen in a storm sewer. It wouldn't be very fun to explain to people that you could have been the champion, except for a little underground detour you took, and then they'd ask where and laugh their heads off when you told them!

When Papa was in the Forest Service, he and his friends sang a song that went, "A man lay down by the sewer, and by the sewer he died. The coroner gave his verdict. They called it 'Sewer Side.'"

That's bad enough, but can't you just imagine all the jokes people will tell her? I bet lots of people will ask her, "Was it smelly, Nelly?"

Maybe I was supposed to fall out of the cave. I don't think it was because Gunn was mad about me throwing out his bones. I know the real reason. It's like the note from Morgan said. I got feeling all important. And I thought it wouldn't matter how it looked to other people; I even said it out loud. So that's why.

When I got to sing my solo part with the glee club, I practiced where the acoustics was best, in the bathroom. It sounded really and truly like a cathedral. Maybe it helps to remember unimpressive stuff like that about our accomplishments so we aren't tempted to put on airs.

I didn't get any musical ability from my parents, but I still can't help wondering if I could be a really good singer someday. I just read where Lady Catherine de Bourgh said, "If I had ever learnt, I should have been a great proficient." I kind of think that way too, but I can't say it, because it sounds too braggy.

Anyway, maybe that's why I fell. Because I forgot we practiced in the girls' bathroom and I took Nelly's place in the spelling bee, and because I had it in my mind that maybe I could have been a great proficient. And because of pretending, which is like the "L" word. I'll just say it. It's like lying.

If I ever was really good someday, Mother and Papa would tell me I was wonderful, but they wouldn't really know the difference! I'd really rather not get credit for things when I don't deserve it, because then it seems like it shouldn't count the rest of the time either.

I love Olive Witch forest, and I love talking with you. Maybe this is the place I belong most of all. Guess what I

Maybe this is the place I belong most of all.

found on the way! A box turtle who doesn't think I'm impor-
tant. He wasn't at all awestruck, and he didn't even bother to
pull his head in the shell. He seemed like he was trying to spell
airplane, which is especially challenging for a turtle, except he
was doing it with charades. I held him up and he kept trying
to demonstrate flying, so we had a conversation about how fun
that would be. Although I did most of the talking.

What if every time I got proud my ears would grow, like
happens to Pinocchio's nose when he lies. Actually I'd like it if
I could fly like Dumbo!

Hetty spotted a flying squirrel. Never having seen one before, she left Hannah, and eagerly followed it to the best of her
ability. It was clever enough to be on the other side of the tree
at all times. Soon their game of hide and seek became a game
of hide and give up, but not entirely from lack of persistence.
Hetty had spotted a beautiful parula warbler flitting after insects. She followed it for some distance and watched the tiny
blue, olive and yellow acrobat hang upside down from a twig.

One discovery led to another, until Hetty was surprised to
find she had come to a small stone cottage. The garden that
skirted it was enclosed by a white picket fence. It was a welcoming sight, with tall pink hollyhocks and yellow climbing
roses on either side of the gate.

Hetty valued her own privacy and respected the privacy of
others; however, the gate itself seemed to be expecting her, as
if it had been purposely left ajar, hoping to draw her in. The
path under her feet was of carefully fitted stones with baby
tears and soft green mosses in the chinks, and it led her to a
French door directly ahead.

The sun, shining through rippled panes of glass, illuminated a small bedroom with a stone fireplace. A violin lay

upon the simple white counterpane covering the bed.

Hetty, turning to leave, began to realize how inappropriate it had been to make herself so welcome. Just then the light fell on a photograph visible from both the bed and the garden. She was chilled by what she saw. The photograph in the frame was of her face.

What could this mean?

She heard a scuffling sound coming from the other side of the house, so she ran as quietly as possible and hid behind a rain barrel, hoping to avoid detection. While waiting for a chance to run away, she heard the sound of breaking glass, and afterward sensed a figure darting into the thicket beyond the yard.

As soon as Hetty felt it was safe to make her escape, she headed back along the path she had followed through the gate when entering the yard. Suddenly the glint of broken glass startled her. Upon hearing the shards of glass crunch beneath her boots, she stopped. Glancing through the shattered panes of the French door, her body stiffened at what she discovered. Her photograph had been stolen!

Mother and Papa would know what to do, but they were still at work. Hetty ran toward the library. She would tell Marian about it. The closest telephone was there.

Marian wasn't at the library, but her assistant said Hetty could use the telephone. Hetty thought Melinda might give her the courage to call the police and report the crime, so she dialed her at OL 2216. Melinda wasn't home, but Morgan answered the phone.

"Maybe you'd rather not be involved. I'll go over there if you want," he reassured her. Hetty was relieved to know Morgan would take care of it now.

The Past Revisited

Leaf's thoughts carried him back to a time three years earlier, when his sister Freydis had just lost her husband. Leaf had known she was going to need him. He and Freydis had moved into a little stone cottage they had chosen together. He would miss the students he had been teaching at the university, but welcomed the pleasant living arrangement. His sister had always been good company.

The two of them had made music together from the time he was five years old. The age difference of twenty years had melted away many years ago, in the warmth of their affection for one another. There had been the recitals where they played their Bach and Chopin favorites, as well as late nights of fiddling and foot-stomping blue-grass music. They both loved jazz improvisation and experimenting with homemade sound effects.

Soon after he and Freydis moved into the cottage, Leaf had felt drawn to the deep woods. His experience on the subject of invasive plants led him to explore the area surrounding their home, to see what native growing things might encroach on their garden. But most of all he wanted to find the tall trees he had seen in the distance, their leaves shimmering with silver whenever the breezes blew in from the ocean.

As he passed under the high canopy of the forest and made his way through the thicket, Leaf was drawn to the beams of light filtering through the lacy foliage ahead. When he spread apart the branches that bowed over his path, a broad view opened before him.

Near the middle of an unexpected clearing was a scene of such near perfection Leaf almost forgot to breathe. Encircling the greater portion of the opening, he saw a large symmetrical arc of mushrooms. To magicians and poets through the ages, fairy rings such as this one had been both omens of good luck and symbols of lost love. As he opened the curtain of foliage, it was as if he had stepped into the magic of ancient legend or linked his dreams with folklore through the ages.

The fairy ring was sure to shrivel and disappear by tomorrow, and the dry leaves would soon hide all traces of them. When the fairies had danced, the only witness to the event and to the resulting circle would have been the magnificent oak tree now standing over it.

Leaf could now understand the reason behind the many mystical explanations. As a scientist, he would forever remember the beauty of the scene, and he marveled at this work of nature in his own way.

His next few days were busy ones. Furniture that had been put in the wrong places had to be reshuffled. The piano promised to complain unless moved out of the direct afternoon sun. It needed to be placed so he would have room to play the violin next to Freydis without knocking over the lamp with his bow.

Up in the loft, the guestroom needed a window box so guests could pick flowers from the open window. The wrought-iron latch on the front gate needed oiling, and the bluebird house would need to be secured to the picket fence that enclosed the garden. The ivy that arched over the front door required a little trimming, though not enough to disturb the family of sparrows nesting in it.

Leaf tilled the soil where Freydis was planning to put her butterfly garden and then dug another bed just for the pleasure of seeing the fertile soil and the plentiful worms that had

done most of the work for him. A phoebe perched boldly on
the handle of his shovel, flicking its tail impatiently and waiting for his boots to kick up more gnats for its lunch.

The elk-leather boots Leaf wore were caked with mud.
He'd had the boots for fifteen years. Every time he laced
them or greased them, he thought of the time he and his
friends Zack and Dan had all bought their boots together
from White's Boot Company. Though expensive, they had
proven to be essential and had worn like iron in the Forest
Service and in the years since then.

Leaf stopped to mop his forehead and wondered if somewhere Dan might be lacing his boots at this very moment.
Every day there were the same questions: How much time
did Dan and Dora have with Annette? How long had she
lived, or was she still living? Although his life was full and
interesting, every day Leaf hoped he might someday learn of
his daughter.

If anyone had been able to predict Leaf's rapid emotional
recovery after Anne's death, the baby might not have gone to
Dan and Dora. The fate of his child was on Leaf's mind now
as always. Yet there were enough books to be read, trails to
hike, plants and trees to study, that his life went on in a reason-
able enough way that he considered it satisfying, except for
the gap where his wife and daughter should have been.

Pulling off his leather gardening gloves, Leaf planned to
spend some time this afternoon looking at the tree he'd seen
near the fairy ring. He stretched his tall frame and whistled
back to a cardinal that called from the edge of the wood. The
woodland creatures had wandered freely here for years, and
he hoped they would soon become comfortable with human
intruders.

As Leaf approached the bright clearing this time, he sensed a need for caution. He mustn't frighten the deer or whatever it was he thought he saw through the trees. There was movement in the dappled light ahead, then stillness. And again there was a slight motion of something that reflected the sunlight. In order to remain concealed from the creature so near him, Leaf stretched his long legs silently across the ferns, and slowly leaned forward to look through the branches.

He knew her the moment he saw her. The way her soft hair made a peak on her forehead; the dimple in her chin; the pale eyelashes that rimmed her eyes; her blue eyes. They were the color of the sky on a perfect day.

Leaf remembered the blue of the sky one perfect day long ago. Anne had been lying next to him in the grass to watch the clouds change from elephants into hats or funny faces. Just by opening her pale eyelashes, Anne had made the blue of her eyes available to all of heaven that day.

Everything about the child enchanted Leaf: the way she stooped to pick up a twig, her knobby knees sticking out like those of a Daddy-long-legs; the tangles of her hair which caught flecks of sunlight and floated light as milkweed around her; the way she puffed out her pink cheeks, now moist from exertion. She held the corners of a brightly flowered scarf, or maybe a tablecloth, which she swirled in circles around her knees and over her head, laughing and sometimes falling down on her sharp little elbows.

In a voice pure and clear, she began to sing, directing her musical conversation toward the branches of the magnificent tree above her. As she danced around the massive trunk, she allowed her words to tumble over one another, inventing themselves in joy or silliness to suit the changing tune.

Leaf sensed this place needed to be hers alone. But if ever she should need his protection, he would be nearby; nothing could keep him from watching over her.

He smiled at the unruly leather laces and the sturdy bulk of her boots that seemed to anchor her thin legs to the forest floor. There was no mistaking her for a light-footed fairy, dancing in a mystical ring of mushrooms! Leaf knew those boots well; they were like his own.

Annette was alive after all, and she was the most beautiful child he had ever seen. He must not reveal himself to her.

These were some of the thoughts running through Leaf's mind. He often looked back in this way since discovering his daughter so near. He had been watching over her now for three years. During that time he found it necessary to spend much of his time in quiet solitude; if he had circulated openly in such a small town, Annette's family would have learned of his presence, and the happiness of the Lawrence family must never be compromised. He would do nothing that might weaken their bonds.

Leaf had thought it best not to involve Freydis in his complicated feelings. Leaf also knew she would generously urge him to go back to his life as it had been. Freydis would undoubtedly insist she would be fine alone even though Leaf could tell she needed him.

Freydis would soon be going to England to see a series of Shakespeare plays. Leaf was glad for her; it was a trip she had dreamed of for many years, and it was a pleasure to watch her excitement as she worked out every detail. She even planned to leave the evening before and sleep at the school for a speedy departure the next day. The continued happiness of Freydis was just one of many reasons he thought it had been best to spare her.

Freydis had often said that when Leaf was a child she could sense his sadness by looking into his eyes. Now that he was a man, could she still recognize his melancholy? Maybe it was a veiled happiness. He hardly knew what to call his emotions. Leaf hoped she didn't sense how his own secrecy tormented him.

Call Me Flora

Freydis would have gladly raised her brother's child herself, but she was not married at the time of Anne's death, nor did she see any prospects for marriage. On the recommendation of friends, she asked an excellent and sympathetic attorney named John Fairburn to prepare the adoption papers.

Mr. Fairburn had addressed Freydis as "Mrs." when she first graced his office. In time, her unmarried status came to his attention only because she had been hoping so fervently that it would.

The discovery that Freydis was actually an unclaimed jewel caused Mr. Fairburn to twist the corners of his mustache, thinking she might not notice the twitch in his cheek before he became any more flushed. Here she was, the most important person ever to happen to him, and he had no idea how to communicate with her unless he could use business-like words such as *"res ipsa loquitur"* or "notary public."

It was a year before Mr. Fairburn could muster the confidence normally evident in his professional life to invite Freydis out for a candlelight dinner. By the time the taxi had delivered them to the restaurant, Mr. Fairburn was so discombobulated he seemed to have forgotten how to count money. In the muddle of dropping coins and apologizing for stepping on her white shoes, he left behind the bouquet of yellow roses he had hidden next to the driver to surprise her.

Freydis was afraid in his condition he could even forget how to say her name, so to make it easier for him, she said, "I will always remember you brought me a floral bouquet, Mr. Fairburn, if you will call me Flora."

Blithering through dinner, he tipped his goblet of ice water onto her new blue silk dress with the pearl buttons while trying to feel under the table inconspicuously for his lost napkin with his toes. Over the chocolate mousse, which was provided free because his shaking hands had tipped the Cherries Jubilee onto her sleeve, he unfurled a contract he had prepared.

He felt more relaxed now, thinking perhaps a few familiar legal phrases like, *"sine qua non"* and *"ex post facto"* might fit naturally into the conversation. As Freydis was examining the contract, Mr. Fairburn gathered all the courage of his legal convictions to look into her soft gray eyes. When she had read Section 1., subsection c., requesting that Freydis Locke agree to change her name to Freydis Fairburn, she put her hand on his and asked, "Where do I sign?"

Aside from a brief period when she had been teaching school some distance away, Leaf and Freydis had remained as near one another as possible, and in the years after Freydis was married to John Fairburn, Leaf was always welcome in the Fairburn home.

John continued to call her Flora, as it was the name created specially for him at an important moment. From that time on she found the name Flora to be more convenient in her professional life as well, and Leaf usually addressed her that way in the presence of John.

Whether Flora and Leaf were playing the violin and piano, or spoons and washboard, John could not have been a more appreciative or a less discriminating audience. Even during his long and debilitating illness toward the end of his life, and long after he had lost the energy to think and talk, John still had the desire to listen and applaud. He could visualize their performing at Carnegie Hall.

In the final days of his life, Freydis asked him where he wanted to be buried. John had turned up one corner of his mouth in a crooked little smile and whispered to her, "Just surprise me, Flora Dear."

Leaf had many good memories of John and Freydis, who had been his only family for years and years.

CHAPTER ELEVEN

School Ends

Finally it was the last day of school. The girls all opened the lids of their desks to remove the contents. Hetty watched as Melinda's desk spewed forth a tortoise shell comb, a Superman pencil sharpener, one scissor blade, a leaky fountain pen, a bottle of blue ink, one thumbtack, and a picture of Elizabeth Taylor with a horse. Among Melinda's five-cent candies were some cinnamon toothpicks and a half empty box of Jujubes. Hetty wondered if next year's occupant might come complete with the same trappings, right down to the Double Bubble cartoons and Cracker Jack squirt ring. She thought:

The stuff in everybody's desk looks absolutely positively interchangeable. What if we all tied our desks shut till next fall? By then, nobody would remember that it wasn't their own stuff. We'd save lots of time today that we could use to find out our summer reading list instead.

We're just like magpies and bowerbirds; they don't care what they collect either. Their stuff just has to be bright and shiny to impress other birds. That can't be why Melinda kept her broken scissor; it's probably for scraping bubble gum off the lid of her desk.

Hetty pictured a row of magpies blowing bubblegum. About the time her thoughts began wandering even more absently, Mrs. Sapworthy invaded the classroom. The history teacher stood before the blackboard armed with an ominous loose-leaf binder labeled, "Seeking After Opportunities for Personal Growth." The contents of the binder were designed to spell doom for everyone's summer plans. As all eyes followed her, a heavy silence filled the room, punctuated with thunder from the darkening sky.

Just as Mrs. Sapworthy's long purple fingernails were about to open the binder, there came a dramatic rescue. Hetty thought if they had been living in a comic book world, there would have been one of those speech bubbles in the air above them, framing a gigantic "KaPow!" And there would be some flashes and spikes bolting out from it, to show how it was really and truly better than even Superman could have done.

What happened was Mrs. Fairburn. She had come to the rescue just in time. As she entered, her soft gray eyes calmed the room, so that even Mrs. Sapworthy appeared relieved as she closed her black binder.

Mrs. Fairburn reached into her satchel and produced a well-worn copy of *Winnie-the-Pooh*. "This occasion calls for a story," she said, choosing to begin with chapter six.

"IN WHICH EEYORE HAS A BIRTHDAY AND GETS TWO PRESENTS," she began. Hetty had always loved this book. Her father sometimes read it aloud before a crackling fire in the fireplace. She would lie on the rug to listen while her mother did hand stitching. But it was more than the memories of her own hearth that made the present moment so pleasurable. It was being allowed to enjoy the simplicity of the words in a room where normally so much effort was required, and it was good to feel safe and dry while she watched the rain beating against the windows.

Hetty tried not to think about her photograph in the cottage window and how it had been stolen. Maybe Melinda was right, and she was destined to be the strange man's next mummy. She concentrated on remembering the pages of *Winnie-the-Pooh*. With her eyes closed, she could see the little ink drawings of the giant beech tree in the Hundred Acre Wood.

Hetty listened attentively to every word Mrs. Fairburn read. After Piglet had given the gloomy Eeyore a broken balloon for his birthday, and Pooh had given him a pot that no longer had honey in it, Hetty waited for the familiar words she knew would follow.

Hetty detected a slight change in Mrs. Fairburn's voice. It was as if Eeyore had reminded her of someone she cared about who was sad. Maybe someone who was trying to make the best of things. Hetty observed that her eyes were moist and she was definitely trying to hide a lump in her throat.

The wind blew violently now, and the torrential rain was followed by hail. When the school secretary came to the classroom door with a note, Mrs. Fairburn considered the message briefly and announced a new plan. Although the girls had expected to be dismissed by now, they were to stay sheltered inside until the worst of the electrical storm had passed. Normally it was a punishment to be kept after school, but this would be pure adventure! Mrs. Fairburn began reading again. This time, she chose to begin with chapter nine.

"IN WHICH PIGLET IS ENTIRELY SURROUNDED BY WATER," began Mrs. Fairburn. The girls, who were reluctant to be entirely surrounded by water themselves, enjoyed Mrs. Fairburn's choice. As she continued reading, they could imagine Piglet's uneasiness.

At that moment a loud pop sounded and all the lights went out. The afternoon sky became black. Deafening thunder and brilliant flashes of lightning were followed by hailstones as large as marbles. They pelted the windowsills and tore leaves from the trees. The custodian ran up from the basement with matches and candles. Flashlights came from nowhere, transforming pink daytime faces into vampire masks. Many of the girls busied themselves with forming long shadows that crept eerily along the walls. Others practiced being bloodsucking zombies, complete with scientifically correct sound effects.

As a number of bony fingers reached up from the inkwells of the desks, Hetty imagined the room to be the backdrop for a horror movie she would never pay to see. She closed her eyes and put her head on her desk to see if she could make it all go away.

It worked, all right. Soon she pictured herself sitting at her own sunny kitchen table across from a Forest Service Bear by the name of Smokey-the-Pooh. Smokey was a furry fellow outfitted with a shovel and hardhat. Much like Pooh Bear, Hetty's guest certainly wouldn't mind having a little something to eat about now. In no time at all, he was in ecstasy with his own plate of oatmeal cookies and the jug of honey she placed before him.

"Could I trouble you for a fork?" Smokey asked, in a suddenly mournful tone. Smacking his lips, he took the fork between his claws then hummed gratefully, as he dug the tines into his itchy back. The table vibrated with the rumbling of contentment deep in his throat. After the last sticky cookie crumb had disappeared, Hetty and Smokey-the-Pooh headed for the Hundred Acre Wood to collect their friend Piglet along the way.

We'll have to keep Piglet absolutely and positively dry, up in Hannah's branches. I wonder how he could ever dry out, since he's stuffed with sawdust. At least he wasn't filled with anchovies or something disgusting like that, when he was made.

She opened one eye a slit to check on the zombies around her. Just then the lights came on again, and there were audible sighs of relief. The girls gathered their belongings and prepared to leave.

Mrs. Fairburn returned to her office and called a cab. She had packed ahead and slept there at Haxton, so she could go straight to the airport headed for England, the minute school was out.

By the time the taxi came for Mrs. Fairburn, the sun was just beginning to peek through the clouds. Before long, the world outside was pronounced safe, and the school buses lined up to await the girls.

Alone

Stepping off the bus, Hetty looked up the long hill that led to her house. She saw several uprooted trees lying across the long, narrow driveway. An empty police car, unable to pass through the litter of fallen branches, had been abandoned in the grass at the side. Its doors had been left open and the radio crackled. Hetty's stomach churned as she saw the gray corpses of the once noble elm trees now stripped of their former dignity.

Hetty thought of when she had seen a dead possum. It had been hit by a car and was covered with blood. Hoping to move the creature from the pavement to a nicer resting place on the grass, she stepped away to find a strong stick with which to move it. Before she returned, the possum had disappeared.

As she walked up the hill, Hetty carefully picked her way through the mangled branches and telephone wires felled by the tornado. She kept wishing the elm trees were playing possum, and that she could step away for just a moment, and suddenly the elms would stop pretending to be dead.

Hetty had to watch every step until she reached the curve near the top. When she found herself in an unexpected opening, she raised her eyes to see an unfamiliar flat stretch of rubble where her house should have been. The sight sickened her, and she felt the air being sucked out of her. Suddenly her legs seemed almost unattached and wooden.

The trees that had once framed the sea were sheared off at the ground, exposing a vast expanse of deep blue water. Everything that was once familiar to Hetty had disappeared. The tornado had razed the narrow swath of the hilltop, and she could see it had decimated another area on high ground in the distance. There was no evidence of her tree house with its bright curtains. Gone were the little blue shutters she and Papa had made for the windows. The ocean had claimed the adjacent hillside, which now floated away as clusters of debris.

Around the place where her house once stood, Hetty could see a policeman with a gold front tooth. He was putting up "No Trespassing" signs. Groups of people stood clustered around the gaping hole of the exposed basement, like the paper dolls she used to prop up along the edges of her bed. The red vice Papa had clamped to the workbench caught her eye. Some of her scattered schoolbooks were on it, too. She had left them the last thing before school, when she realized she wouldn't be using them. With plaster and dust on them, they looked eerie now.

"Mother and Papa will know what we're supposed to do now," she told herself.

A woman with bobby pins and rollers in her hair approached the policeman. Over and over, she asked the same questions. Annoyed, he stopped his work to glare directly at her. He flashed his gold tooth and, with finality said, "Yes, Ma'am....a wedge tornado." Then, as if through a blurry dream, Hetty heard him continue, "That's right, Ma'am. No one could have survived."

Hetty froze in place, staring like all the paper dolls. "Mother and Papa were waiting for me to come home from school. They would have been here when it happened."

Hetty backed away from the rubble. She ran blindly, tripping and stumbling, her legs still moving like wooden stumps, until she had reached Hannah.

In Hannah

In the past, Hetty had found comfort in Hannah's welcoming branches. Now she felt nothing. Her heartbroken sobs received no solace. As a wave of nausea overcame her she leaned over to vomit, but nothing came up. She sobbed until there were no more tears. In place of the love she had once felt in this place, there was only emptiness.

At the base of the trunk, where it emerged from the soil, she had sometimes found nuts or pretty stones, or a perfect leaf. It was almost as if someone who loved her was telling her so, with simple gifts. Once Hetty had left a note saying, "Whoever you are, I love you," just in case they were from a real person. Nothing was there now.

From habit, her fingers felt for her handkerchief, which she hadn't seen since her fall. She had a faint memory of it slipping from her hand while she was being carried. Maybe her rescuer had paused to retrieve it, but she hadn't seen it since then.

She thought back to a hot summer day when she had been small. Mother had made fresh lemon ice cream in the churn, and Papa was turning the crank for what Hetty considered absolutely and positively the longest time ever. Over and over she asked him when it would be ready. Papa suggested the initials on her handkerchief, "H.A.L." ought to stand for, "Have a Little (blank)," and would she fill in the blank word at the end?

He was waiting for her answer to be, "Patience," but instead, she asked hesitantly if the word might be "Lick." Papa honked his nose and laughed so hard he could hardly crank the bucket, and when it was ready, he handed her the dasher so she could "Have a Lick."

In the past, Hetty had found comfort in Hannah's welcoming branches.

Hetty wondered what to do next, with all this emptiness. Maybe she was supposed to fill in the blank. Should she finish it with the word, "Courage?" Have a Little Courage? Where would courage come from? she wondered.

She didn't know how to think, so she just talked to Hannah.

Pinky always knew what she was supposed to do. Her job was mainly wagging her tail, even when it made trouble the way she wagged it. Like when she wagged the candy dish off the coffee table. It was absolutely and positively Mother's most favorite wedding present because it caught the light and sent all these beams of rainbow colors up on the ceiling at just the right time in the afternoon when everybody could do with a good rainbow. Well, Pinky wagged it clean off the coffee table, and kept right on wagging even after she broke it in a million little shards. We forgave her because she was just doing her job.

I wish I could sleep right now, so I'd feel better in the morning… it's so dark…

What's my job, I wonder…like maybe to keep on wagging my tail…

I wish you could talk to me, Hannah. I used to almost think you could, but I don't feel that way now. You can't hug me back like you used to. I have to keep talking to you anyway. That way I won't have to think.

On one side of the kitchen, when the light switch goes up, it turns the light on. And then on the other side, when it goes up it turns the dark on. I wonder why we don't ever say we "turn on the dark."

Papa said all over the world, people would telegram or telephone somebody to say they love them if they were dying. But we wouldn't need to, because we already know it, even if we didn't just barely say it.

I wish I could tell them again anyway, even if I don't need to. I need their arms around me…and they're gone.

If I can't stop crying, maybe I'll end up like jellyfish do after they dry out in the sun till they're just paper thin like a piece of cellophane. Then if you held me up to the light, you'd see right through me, because there wouldn't be anything in there anymore.

I wish the dark wouldn't ever get turned on …but today the brightness gave me a headache, and it hurt kind of like when a sharp cracker gets caught in your throat. At least the dark doesn't hurt my eyes.

If I still had Pinky, I could put my arms around her and she would drum her tail on the floor. Then even if she couldn't hug me back, I'd know she was in there, wanting to.

When she died, I was on the kitchen floor with my left arm around her neck. She drummed her tail on the linoleum just once. …Well, maybe half a time. Then she got still, and she seemed really heavy. How did she get heavier by dying? In one tiny second, she got turned into nothing but fur and skin… and her collar that said, "Pin-y," because the "k" fell off years ago.

So she wasn't in there any more. It's like the only part that mattered was the light part that had up and floated away, just leaving the rest of her that used to shed hair and click its toenails on the wood floor, and throw up, like when she found my box of chocolate bars.

Is that the way it happened with Mother and Papa? The part of them that would be still and heavy…that's what used to get sunburned…and the part that was their toenails that used to get so thick Papa said he ought to save them to shingle the roof. And especially the part that limped, and the part of them that always needed deodorant and wondered why it was all used up.

It's the light part that's going to be them forever. It's so light that I'm afraid it'll float away, if I don't keep it in my head. Like the way Mother sang so off key that you didn't know what she was singing till she'd filled in enough words.

I wonder if there will ever be a perfect day again. I had a perfect day once when we were outside and Mother brought out the material she bought that I'd cut from the pattern, and she put my Featherweight sewing machine in the sunshine on the back patio, with a long extension cord that went in through the Dutch door in the kitchen, so there was a little crack where an inchworm got in, and we let it crawl up and down our arms.

It would get down to the end of my finger and think, "Where did the world go?" and turn around and go up again. It didn't ever figure out the particular world it was on. Then I moved its world so I could get on with making the most useful nightgown ever.

I guess it's kind of like that with me. The world I used to be on got all moved around. Am I going to have to get used to it?

Papa says we're not just made of the things that happen to us. When something happens, it's what we do about it that matters most. What I better do about it is think.

The Board Game

When I was little, a friend of Mother's brought her son over to play a board game with me. He kept saying, "I'll tell you what I'm gonna do," then he'd wait for me to ask, "What?" which I didn't, so he'd answer himself, "I'm gonna tell you what I'm gonna do. That's what I'm gonna do," and on and on like that till the game never got anywhere. Board games never do, any-way, because the tiny pieces you move around on them have to stay right there in their little squares.

I suppose that's where I am right now.

A really good game should make it possible for the little pieces to be put in a kayak or an airplane heading for Mt. Mc-Kinley or Cape Town, South Africa.

I want to do like in the dreams I sometimes have, when I work really hard flapping my arms until I'm perspiring all over, so if I was Papa I would for sure be searching through all the drawers for the deodorant and bellowing, "Dorie, where's the Stopette?" but anyway, I flap so hard that if there's any breeze at all, I get up high enough to see the way the world curves away on all sides, and it's so bright that it ought to hurt like crackers, but it doesn't. And I want to keep going higher, and getting closer to the light, and it gets brighter and brighter, until the perfect day.... I can keep hoping I'll dream I'm flying over and over again. But that's just a dream, and I want something that's real to be just as good as that. So now what am I supposed to do about what's happening?

Miracle Wings

Once we found a dead bird that flew hard against the window and broke its neck. Papa held it in both his hands and its head hung down pitifully between his fingers. Mother and I spread his wings all the way open, and they were absolutely perfect. The sun made the gray feathers turn blue and gold and green, and the feathers fanned out like they were miracles even though he was dead and couldn't use his wings for flying any more. But they weren't wasted, because we got to see what a miracle looks like up close.

Maybe you've kind of been like my board game, Hannah. And maybe I need to get off. I guess whatever I do next would be better if I'm with people. The longer I put it off, the harder… still, I sometimes wish I could be like Hallie Daggett. Everyone back in 1913 thought she was going to be all whiney and say she was scared of the loneliness and mountain lions, and things like that. She watched for fires from Eddy Gulch Lookout on Klamath Peak for a whole fourteen years. She was the first woman ever to be a lookout for the Forest Service, and one of the very best ever. That's why I wrote a report about her, so I could be more like that.

In the morning, I'll go to the library. Miss Reed is surrounded by imagination, so she might know what I'm supposed to do. There are so many books all around her with millions of amazing words in them. Even after people are as dead as a dead bird, I can still read the words they wrote. They're so full of dreams and possibilities, it's like they've left their miracle wings still spread out.

Hetty had knocked out a section of the ledge just below her cliff cave. She could feel safe staying in her hideaway now, without fearing the approach of Gunn or any other animal by that route. Knowing she needed strength to face the next morning, she tried to sleep.

She longed to dream she was flying, as if by soaring over herself she could get a clearer picture of what was real and what was not, but the dream became an exhausting effort in which she pumped her arms until the sweat matted her hair and mixed with her tears. She curled up in the leaves and held her knees to try to control the shaking.

Her nose was running, and she wanted her handkerchief. She had tissues somewhere, but the half moon didn't provide enough light for her to find them. Leaves were stuck to her face and in her hair. The mosquitoes whined around her, so she pulled her flowered tablecloth over her face and arms, which left her legs exposed.

Hetty thought of how bats could eat a thousand mosquitoes in an hour. She and Papa had built a bat house, but someone who thought he was being helpful destroyed it and killed all the bats and their pups. Papa said not to be angry, because a lot of people are just misinformed by seeing too many Halloween movies. He said sometimes thoughtless people disturb bats in their caves just to see them fly around. That can kill them, because they need sleep in order to live.

Hetty began to sob again, as the thought of the cruel death of the bats added further to her sorrow. In her heavy sadness Hetty felt fragile too, and wondered if her disturbed sleep could cause her life to ebb as well.

CHAPTER TWELVE

The Courtroom

Morning came as it always does. Hetty had hoped with the start of a new day everything would be as it used to be. But nothing had changed since the previous night; she was still alone.

As she stirred in her nest, Hetty felt determined to be thankful that nothing about the day had gone wrong yet. She stretched her spine, picked out the leaves she felt in her hair, and straightened her clothing as well as she could.

It was hard to think what possibilities lay ahead of her. Still, Hetty fully expected to find comfort in the company of Miss Reed. Marian had known Mother, and would understand why Hetty missed her so.

When it seemed about time for the library to open, Hetty reached the front entrance. But before pulling open the door, she saw Marian entering a public building down the block. Hetty quickly followed after her into the building and through a series of doors. Once inside, Hetty thought it likely she would see Marian inside the one door that was still ajar.

Through the door she saw a flag at the front and a solemn-faced judge presiding over the setting. Hetty tiptoed to the only available seat near the back where she had entered. The slightest sounds seemed amplified by the formality the room required. Marian was sitting close to the front. As Hetty could see no way to get her attention, she would have to wait patiently for the end of whatever was about to happen. Hetty sensed that just before her arrival some sort of orders for respectful silence had been given.

The Preliminary Hearing

Hetty sat and watched and waited. For some time, a tall man with kind gray eyes had been the center of her attention. He was seated just in front of a policeman. As he appeared to be deep in thought, she was able to observe him closely. He reminded Hetty of Mrs. Fairburn. Hetty always felt things would turn out as they should just by looking into her eyes.

"Those concerned with the matter of Leaf Locke please come forward and take your places," said the judge.

Hetty knew she had heard the name "Leaf" before. "The man who saved Papa's life was named Leaf too," she thought.

The tall man, followed by the policeman, rose from his seat to approach the judge. As he did so, he surprised Hetty by looking in her direction. She was certain that he was startled at the sight of her. Maybe it was because she looked untidy.

No, she was sure that wasn't the reason. When his eyes met hers, it was as if he knew her, yet he had quickly and deliberately averted his eyes to deny the fact.

"This is a preliminary hearing," the judge told the man. We are holding it the day after your arrest to determine whether there is sufficient evidence to hold you in jail. If there is, an arraignment will follow, at which time you will be able to enter a plea of guilty or not guilty.

"Are you represented by an attorney, Mr. Locke?" asked the judge.

"No, Your Honor."

"I will reset this hearing for five days from now, during which time you must find an attorney," the judge said.

As Hetty was listening for the man to respond, someone entered the courtroom and stepped forward to get the judge's attention. He spoke confidently and with the respect required by the surroundings.

In a clear voice, he said, "May it please the court, I'm an attorney authorized to practice in this jurisdiction. I'm a long-time friend of the defendant, though we haven't been in contact for fifteen years. May I have ten minutes with Mr. Locke, to see if he may wish me to represent him?"

The attorney looked old and tired, but very much like Papa. Hetty longed for her beloved papa when she saw him.

Then her eyes widened, and she heard herself cry, "Papa," with quiet excitement. He was really there. In the same room! Papa didn't seem to see her.

Was Mother there too? If so, she would be too small to see in the crowd.

Hetty could hardly hold still with all the joy that was welling up inside her. It was like her throat wanted to be in charge of the excitement; it wanted to yell across the crowd and take her with it and make a proclamation for everyone to hear:

Stop whatever you're doing! The king of all the Papas in the whole entire world is alive, and we're all going to dance while he gives me the tightest hug there could ever be. And now everybody help me find Mother!

Hetty saw Papa approach the tall man they called Leaf and embrace him.

The man directed Papa's attention in Hetty's direction.

Their eyes met and suddenly she saw love written all over his face. Where his expression had been tired and listless just a moment ago, Papa now seemed young and animated by the relief of seeing her.

He wiped some tears then honked his nose several times, for sheer joy. His eyes sought her repeatedly as if to make sure of her presence. It was clear he wanted to come to her, yet Hetty understood there was some kind of real importance to what he was doing.

All of a sudden Hetty noticed Morgan sitting next to the policeman. It was odd that he was there. She hadn't noticed him before. What did it all mean?

Was that the man she and Morgan had reported as a thief? Could that be Papa's friend Leaf?

Marian turned around and brightened with surprise as she saw Hetty, then rushed to be with her at the back of the room.

"Annette!" she said in a loud library whisper. Marian squeezed the breath out of her. "I can hardly believe it's you. This will make everyone so happy! We thought you'd been taken out to sea."

Hetty decided a librarian was the perfect person to represent all the others who couldn't get away with violating the silence.

Case Dismissed

"You must speak up in your own defense, Leaf," Hetty heard Papa say.

"I've tried to stay in the background for the three of you," replied the tall man with concern.

"I believe Hetty is ready to know everything now," Papa replied.

At the preliminary hearing, the judge needed to know what had led to Leaf's arrest for burglary. He learned the sequence of events as Papa explained it:

"Your Honor, may it please the court… it seems Mr. Leaf Locke had seen Henrietta Annette Lawrence— this young lady is known as Hetty by her friends or as Annette by her biological Father, Leaf Locke—Mr. Locke had seen Annette approaching his cottage.

"At that time he was not willing to reveal his identity as her father, for fear it would be hurtful to her and her adoptive parents.

"Because Annette looked so much like her natural mother, Anne Locke, Mr. Locke was determined to keep his wife's picture out of her sight. He did not realize Annette had already seen that very portrait through the glass door of his bedroom, and that she had thought it was of her own face.

"He knew there would not be time for him to enter by the front door without Annette's seeing him, so he broke the window of his own bedroom door, reached in and removed the portrait. Subsequently he ran into the woods so she would

not see him or her mother's picture.

"That is where Mr. Morgan Morganthal saw Mr. Locke and was therefore able to identify him.

"Your Honor, I submit that the damage Mr. Locke did was to his own house. The photograph he removed from the window of his own door was a portrait of his deceased wife. The picture already belonged to him.

"Thank you."

"Is it true what your counsel has just told us, Mr. Locke?" asked the judge.

"Yes, Your Honor," came the reply.

The judge pounded his gavel and the case was dismissed.

Dora quickly made her way to the front near Leaf and Dan. She stood on her toes looking for Hetty until Dan lifted her by the waist. When at last she saw Hetty, hers was the happiest face in the room. With her braid hanging down over her right shoulder, there was nothing to hold back the little wisps of her hair that had escaped to dance around her face.

Hetty's thoughts raced with confusion, excitement and joy. It was too much for her to absorb. She had listened carefully in the courtroom, but still didn't fully understand the implications of what she had heard.

Marian gripped her hand. It made Hetty feel safe in spite of the turmoil inside her.

She asked Marian, "Can I stay next to you? I don't see how Mother and Papa can be alive," she puzzled.

She let Marian lead her toward Dan and Dora.

"I know why they thought I was dead!" She said it to herself as much as to Marian. "It was the books. They would've seen my schoolbooks in the basement," she added.

As the eager smiles came toward them she whispered to

Marian, "Papa knew that man before."

Marian thought it best to remain silent.

United

Leaf was flooded with gratitude for Dan and Dora Lawrence who had made this moment possible. He spoke quietly to them.

"For three years I've watched her grow," he said, "with no hope of meeting her."

"To think that you have been here all this time! said Dora.

"She needs to know you now, Leaf. We have always hoped she would," she added.

"Hetty knows exercising love won't use it up. There's more than enough to go around."

"What will she call me?"

"We've been saving the name 'Father' for you," said Dan.

In the Cottage

Mrs. Fairburn looked from the kitchen into the sunroom. Annette was sleeping there, nestled in the daybed, with her yellow hair curling over the pillow. Her cheeks appeared especially pink against the white pillowcase. In the guestroom directly above the sunroom, Flora could hear Dan and Dora just beginning to stir. She continued working in the kitchen as quietly as possible.

Hetty was awakened when a branch of leaves brushed the windowpane, sounding to her like the wings of a bird against the glass. Her eyes opened to a bright and glorious morning as the song of a thrush reached her through the sunroom windows.

With their own home destroyed, this would be their first day in the cottage with her headmistress and Leaf Locke. Hetty thought of the night before:

Mrs. Fairburn had abandoned her Shakespeare adventures without regret to come home from England as quickly as possible. The moment she came in the door she had taken both Hetty's hands in hers.

"Dearest Hetty. Our own Annette," she had said, "there is nothing that could have kept me away."

Hetty looked into the soft gray eyes. Her eyes had spoken her thoughts without any need for words.

"This is a time of such significance, and I'm so very happy for my brother," Mrs. Fairburn had said. "We hope while you're waiting for your home to be built the three of you will feel welcome and comfortable here."

Now it was time to dress and prepare for the new day. Hetty wasn't sure what to do next, but in no time at all, Mrs. Fairburn greeted Hetty warmly and slipped a white ruffled apron over her head. She suggested she come into the kitchen to help put powdered sugar on some hot scones. She had prepared so many scones and such a large pitcher of freshly squeezed orange juice that Hetty wondered how the five of them could possibly eat them all.

It was very pleasant working next to Mrs. Fairburn and talking with her about how a sweet lemon glaze might taste. Looking outside, Hetty saw the legs of a ladder that was being carried around the corner of the house. She watched as Leaf Locke approached whoever was carrying it, and thanked him warmly for whatever he was doing.

Suddenly, Mrs. Fairburn seemed to receive a signal through the window, and she said, "Now you need to see what your friends have made for you." Taking Hetty by the hand, she led her outside through the kitchen door and along the flagstone path to look back at the house.

Hetty had never seen a more festive or joyful banner. In all colors of the rainbow, it said, "We love you Hetty! Keep smiling!" It reached from the corner of the roof to the lamppost.

Morgan was standing by the gate holding the ladder, with a wide grin on his face. He and Melinda had brought Gretchen, Louisa and Sue, who were hiding behind the fence to watch Hetty's reaction. The girls had all joined with Melinda in helping to paint the message.

When they suddenly popped up from behind the fence, Hetty could hardly believe the wonder of it all. She couldn't think of any words to say, but she didn't need to. Melinda, who had anticipated her friend's excitement, felt more than repaid by Hetty's obvious joy.

The girls had all brought some of their clothes to give her. Melinda brought her several bright and cheerful sweaters. One had pink flowers embroidered on each wrist. There were dungarees, skirts and blouses, and a number of other things her friends were parting with so she could have a change of clothes right away.

When Mother and Papa came downstairs, they saw Hetty surrounded by a sort of festive giddiness that was new to her. She seemed overwhelmed by their enthusiasm, unaccustomed as she was to so much attention. Still, it was clear Hetty was glad these were her friends.

Gretchen produced the old party invitation that had

been meant for Hetty. She apologized and explained it had slipped behind the dashboard of their car. Gretchen wanted to show Hetty their own color television some day if they should ever get one.

When the happy chatter ended and the last crumb of scones had been devoured, Morgan took Hetty's visitors away and the kitchen became peaceful again. While Papa went outside to see the banner, Hetty sat with her mother in uncomfortable silence, thinking about how changed her life would be now. She was the only girl in the school who could call her beloved headmistress Aunt Freydis. Hetty began thinking about Louisa, and wondering if she would ever learn about having been adopted. There were friends to learn about, and they were not just make-believe friends. They cared about her.

After a while, Freydis asked Hetty if she would call Leaf in from the yard. Hetty looked out the window and saw that Leaf Locke and Papa were together, engrossed in conversation. She worried:

It would be hard to call him "Leaf," or "Father," even if he asked me to.

How do I call him? If I say, "She wants you," they might both ask, "Which one of us does she want?" Then I'd have to say, "She wants the one I don't call Papa."

Hetty decided to go close enough to look directly in his eyes. That way, when she said "You," he would know who she was talking to. Freydis quickly realized Hetty's predicament, and solved it by calling Leaf herself.

The Album

Mother held a worn white leather album in both her hands. Embossed on the cover was "Henrietta Annette Lawrence," in delicate gold letters.

Mother took Hetty by the hand and seated her on a tuffet in the sunny bay window. They looked out over the pink roses and clematis arching over the white trellis at the gate. The sky was clear blue with little white puffs of clouds that seemed to be peeking in the window so they could see what was in the album.

Mother waited until Hetty seemed ready. She tucked a wandering lock of hair into place and said, "This is for you to give your Father, Hetty."

Hetty looked at Papa, who nodded.

Papa wasn't reaching for the album. It wasn't meant for him. Hetty felt a lump in her throat.

I don't want to open the cover because it would be like saying to Papa that it's okay if he's not my father. And it would be opening a lot of other things I don't understand. I can't do that right now. I wish I could hold it in my lap until the little puffs of clouds force me to show them what's in it; then it wouldn't be my decision.

Mother sat on the window seat. She reached over and encouraged Hetty to open the album cover. The first page had her birth certificate. Hetty thought:

Anne has signed it in really delicate letters. She must have liked doing calligraphy like me. I wonder if she practiced writing her baby's name lots of times or pictured teaching her how to write some day.

Hetty looked at pictures of times she would never forget, and many other photographs she had never seen. There was one of Anne with a ribbon holding back her hair.

Maybe Mr. Locke knows about the album, so it would be rude not to give it to him. But he won't care about my baby pictures.

You are the ones who love me. Why would you want me to give them away? How can we give him the picture of the stepping stool? I made it so you could reach the cabinets. And that one's of me the first time I wore your boots, Papa.

Papa seemed to know Hetty's thoughts. "I owe him my life, and he gave us you," he said. "This will mean more to Leaf than you know, Hetty.

"We hoped some day we could thank him together," Papa said. "That's the reason we've kept this since your birth."

Mother opened the back cover. Attached to it was a soft peach satin pouch she had made. Her small fingers pulled something out. She stood behind Hetty, pulled her hair back, and fastened it with a ribbon. It was blue taffeta, the color of the sky.

Hetty wanted to see Mother and Papa laughing, and eating cookies, and playing Scrabble. She wasn't ready to look like Anne. She wished she could be tiny like her mother, and have the same dark eyes.

"Your Aunt Freydis tells us this was Anne's ribbon.

"For almost fifteen years, you have thought you just belonged to us." Hetty saw tears were filling Mother's eyes.

She thought, "Mother seems happy, but maybe a little confused, the same as me."

Hetty didn't know what to say, so she put her arms around Dora's waist. She could tell her mother was trying to compose herself, but she was shaking inside.

"When you look in the mirror," Dora continued, "you'll see your own image, but you'll be seeing Anne now as well. Always remember you belong to others who love you, too." Hetty tightened her arms around her mother.

Papa honked his nose and winked at her.

CHAPTER THIRTEEN

Thinking Ahead

Over the years Leaf had tried to picture his daughter at every stage of her life. Annette's childhood had sped past without his witnessing any part of it.

Quite suddenly on the day she fell, he realized Annette was becoming a young woman. When he carried her limp body out of the woods, she was no longer the loose collection of bones and angles he had first seen in the forest three years before. She was a woman-child, with the same translucent skin, pale lashes and silken curls as before her surprising transformation.

Holding the photograph album in his lap, Leaf looked at every detail over and over. Lost was her infancy when he could have been her protector and defender. He could no longer rock her to sleep singing a lullaby. He would never see Annette wait for the tooth fairy or play jump-the-rope.

Although nothing would bring back the past, Leaf welcomed his future responsibilities and hoped to exercise them wisely.

He began to imagine Annette in the coming years, arriving home in the evening after a date. He could picture himself at the cottage window awaiting her safe return. He leaned back in his easy chair and considered how it might be:

"She'll give me a hug when she first comes in. Then she'll say, 'Father, Bardolph is a wonderful man, and I'm very much in like with him.'

Leaf raised his eyebrows the way he imagined he would while listening for further information.

She might say, 'He has a very nice voice, and he brings me chocolates. We would like your blessing on our marriage.'

Leaf doubted whether he could ever give his blessing, whether they were deeply in like or not. If ever there was a Bardolph, he couldn't possibly be good enough for her.

"I won't give her away," he thought.

"Oh, wait. It's Dan who would be giving her away. How could Dan do such a thing?" He leaned back again and his thoughts continued.

Maybe I should ask her, 'What does your Papa say?'

She might tease me, and answer, 'Papa says no. That's why I'm asking you.' But she'll really understand it doesn't work that way.

Then I'd have to look into her eyes and explain to her, 'I want you to find someone who loves you as much as I loved your mother.'

That's like saying, when we fly a man to the moon, Father," she'll say. "That's never going to happen either. I might as well plan on being an old maid who collects toilet paper tubes for fun.'

Then she will straighten my tie just the way Anne used to do.

Leaf suppressed a chuckle, and thought of a different approach he might use. He thought:

I may have to be direct. That's probably how Dan would handle it.

I could tell her I'm looking for some small signs of consideration from the boy, and I don't see them in Bardolph.

If I saw Bardolph go straight for the most comfortable chair while Annette is still standing, or something like that, maybe I should point that out.

Or I could tell her, 'My biggest concern is about the way he looks at you. I want to be sure you're important to him in the right way.'

That might make Annette say, 'I guess I know what you mean. It doesn't bother me the way Marian looks all googley-eyed at you, but it would if I didn't like her so much.'

I would insist Marian doesn't look all googley-eyed at me.

Leaf felt the pink color creeping into his cheeks and resolved to stop imagining Marian into the conversation.

Next he pictured Annette tactfully changing the subject:

'Bardolph gave me some of those creamy chocolates with

a cherry inside. You know…the kind that drip down on your chin if you aren't careful.'

'The ones that come in pink and green cellophane?' I'd ask. 'I see. Well, that changes everything!'

I would laugh so she could see I was only joking. Then I would hug her again while she sheds just a few tears.

Leaf wondered if he might also say *I've been waiting for someone who's carrying a pedestal around with him, so he can put you on it,* but he decided he would have said enough already.

He felt sure Annette would take back her request for him to talk to Papa about Bardolph; she would have resolved to set her standards higher.

For three years the mirror had reflected the sadness in Leaf's eyes; he could see it himself, yet if he had to rethink it, he would make the same decision. He had been watching over their daughter for Anne's sake as well, and it had been worth everything. He felt reassured that Dan and Dora were the parents Annette had needed; they were raising her to think wisely. He would have to watch and learn from them.

Leaf was glad so much of Annette's important thinking was still far in the future, and that he could be a part of it. There would still be time for him to enjoy at least a small portion of her childhood.

He put the album down on the table next to Anne's picture. As he did, he saw Annette in the back yard with someone behind her. Leaf had to lean forward to be sure of what he saw.

Morgan had given his crystal set to Annette, since hers had been destroyed by the tornado. Now he was bringing a stand to support it. It was Morgan he saw walking behind Annette, carrying a pedestal.

The Perfect Day

While Mother and Papa were at the office, Aunt Freydis showed Hetty how to cut lilac stems so they would stay fresh longer, and she shared other ideas that were entirely new to Hetty. They filled three vases with deep lavender lilacs, then tucked in some white petunias to trail down the sides.

"You might put this one on the table next to Dan and Dorie's bed," she suggested, "and this one can go on Leaf's dresser." Her soft eyes seemed to become the color of the lilacs in her hand. "And which one would you like in the sunroom, dear?"

After Hetty put one vase in the guestroom and another in the sunroom, she carried the last one to Leaf's dresser and put it next to the picture of Anne.

As Hetty was leaving the room, she stopped at the low table next to Leaf's easy chair. She was puzzled by what she saw there. It was a small picture frame that displayed a note she had written several years ago. She remembered having decorated the message with a blue crayon and then propping it against the foot of Hannah. The note read, "Whoever you are, I love you."

Later, Hetty told Aunt Freydis and Leaf she was going

to walk over to where her home had been. She intended
to watch their house being rebuilt. But when she began
thinking of the many things she had to work out in her
mind, she changed her plans and went instead to Hannah.
She leaned against the back of Hannah's trunk and thought.

*Papa's easy to talk to, so everything's really natural when
we're all together, he and Leaf are such good friends. But
when I'm alone with Leaf, I'm not sure how I'm supposed
to talk to him. I know he's not waiting for Papa's permission
to be my father... Mother and Papa have always said there's
enough love to go around.*

*I have permission to be anything I need to be. But am I
brave enough to be a daughter to someone else? I guess I'm
just afraid of starting all wrong.*

*Papa says it's not that Leaf is being cautious with his af-
fection. He's just being wise and waiting for me to go to him.*

I don't know how.

*I heard about some people in Europe during the war.
They saved their cheese in a glass jar to make it last longer,
and then they took turns licking the outside of the jar. That's
all they got. Maybe that's me, and I'm kind of licking the
outside of the jar. And it's not enough.*

Hetty was sure Hannah understood, but as she hadn't
suggested any answers, Hetty decided she would do better to figure it out back at the cottage. She was standing
to leave. Someone was there, but she had been so deep in
thought that she hadn't seen anyone come. As she stood up
and looked around the trunk, he was there, pressing some-

thing against Hannah's bark.

It was Leaf. She stood very still. He had come with her handkerchief.

Then his kind gray eyes met hers and she felt a quiet peace in the depth of them. Hetty knew him now. It had been Leaf watching over her all this time. Leaf was the tall man who had carried her to safety.

The sun seemed to grow brighter and brighter. She blinked and thought of who she was and what it all meant.

Hetty ran to him. "Father!" she cried.

He held her tight because she was his.

P.S. I Love You, Hannah

Oh, Hannah! If you could only imagine this week! It's better than a dream. And we've even had lots of music. Doesn't it seem like everything sings and flies up to the sun when you're happy? You have wings today too, Hannah!

Hannah seemed to understand. She swayed gracefully, as if to join in all the flying.

Sometimes I forget you're a tree because you listen to everything I say. Sometimes I even learn things from what spills over when we talk. Besides, you make me feel like I can do anything if I work hard enough. Even really hard things.

Mother's friend says if you don't like making pies, you should make seven in a row, so she did it, and now she likes making pies, and she's really good at it, too. I know, because she brought over a pie made with huckleberries she'd picked herself. It was so good, I waited till nobody could see me, and I actually licked my plate.

So I guess I should try to talk to people when it's hard, seven times in a row. I guess it behooves me to at least get better at it. I wish I could line seven people all up in a row and do all seven "How-do-you-do's," one after another. But I couldn't anyway, because if I got tongue-tied, they would find out I couldn't think of anything to say except that it's nice weather, over and over.

Papa says if you really care about people, they'll hear it in your voice so what you say doesn't matter as much as your inside feelings that will come out.

It's like Aunt Freydis. Miss Altoona says she worked in the same school with her for years. She's the only person at Haxton who used to know her as Freydis Locke. She would follow her anywhere, and it's because of how Aunt Freydis cares about everybody. Miss Altoona says she would like to be just like her, so I guess people who aren't even that way themselves can still tell who is.

Anyway, it behooves me to be more sociable. Oh, well... I shouldn't be so busy thinking about getting behooved that I don't actually do anything. Papa says I can either be content to just hear about things that happen, or I can be a happenmaker myself.

The thing is this: when we say, "It's raining," we know that means the rain is raining. But when we say, "It behooves me," we do not mean that behoove is behooving me. I'll ask Papa about it when he gets home. My treasure box is so full of Papa's notes, I'm going to need a new one. If I'd left it in the tree house, it'd be washed out to sea, so it's a good thing I kept it here.

I'm kind of okay with the tree house being gone, because the fun part was mostly building it with Papa and furnishing it with Mother. Like with all the sandcastles we've built; we never visit them again, because it's making something that's the best part.

Maybe it's like we make up ourselves as we go along. But we can't really abandon ourselves when we're done, even if we don't like what we've made. We're kind of stuck with our own selves and who we are when we're through.

Father thinks I don't belong to anyone quite as much as to myself. He says he and Aunt Freydis couldn't have chosen a better home for me.

I never knew Mother had a baby boy that was born early in their marriage, but he died at birth, and she couldn't have any more children. And Father told me about my handkerchief. It's

She swayed gracefully as if to join in all the flying.

a Norwegian kind of lace. He gave it to Anne for their wedding, so that's her initials on it. Their first daughter was always supposed to have those same initials. They planned it that way for sentimental reasons.

We make music absolutely all the time at the cottage. Aunt Freydis is going to teach me to play the piano, and Father says he'll be able to give me lessons, even if he can't find his other violin. He's planning to stay home a lot this summer to be with me. I love being with him. He says Mother and Papa really need to go to work more now, since they had to stay home with me so much when I was little. I never thought about it that way.

Father said he knows a good singer, if I want to have voice lessons, and Mother and Aunt Freydis asked if his name was Bobby. Father laughed when he said it ought to be someone who wouldn't fly south every winter. Actually, whoever Bobby is, I wish he or anyone else could start me right away, even if I'd need another teacher in the winter.

Marian can yodel! She says it's because of her papa. She called him Joey. Joey had to leave suddenly one day because his mother was dying. After he'd gone, Marian's mother wouldn't ever let him come back. But Marian never forgot the fun of hearing Joey yodel. That's how she got started.

Father's been inviting Marian to come talk with me about my reading. She always comes right over, even if she has to bring Gorilla with her. Father must need more advice about books than me, because they go on long walks together. Yesterday when they got back, Gorilla was asleep on Father's shoulder. I asked what books they talked about, and they just smiled and looked at each other, but they couldn't remember any of them. Father said there are an awful lot of books in the library.

Mother told Marian about how Leaf had saved Papa's life

*in a forest fire. She looked a bit dazed for a while. I thought
everybody knew, but I guess Marian didn't. She must not have
noticed the burn scars on Father's arm or Papa's limp.*

*Marian's eyes got all teary, and she told Mother, "You've
saved my life, Dorie. You and your family."*

*I wasn't sure what she meant, but Mother explained that
Marian's still learning to trust people. Till she met us, she had
to learn about families by reading books. I'm glad I didn't have
to learn that way, because of Mother and Papa.*

*Papa doesn't scatter crumbs on purpose, and Mother tries
to sweep them up so no one will notice. She also keeps up the
supply of razor blades so Papa won't have to borrow them from
Father like he always had to do when they were in the Forest
Service.*

*Thursday night, Father asked Freydis what we'd be having
for dinner, and Aunt Freydis said, "Cuckoo Fricasee," and I
thought, oh, no! I knew what she was saying. She'd found my
dead bird in the Frigidaire!*

*I was saving a beautiful cuckoo that had flown into the
window. I put him in a big glass jar in the refrigerator so I could
show Mother and Papa, but I didn't mean it to still be there by
dinnertime. And you know what? I could tell Aunt Flora didn't
mind at all. She and Father were excited to admire it too.*

*I guess Father's just extra good at being forgiving. Morgan
was afraid he would be furious about the two of us turning him
in to the police, but we didn't know what he was like then.
Morgan didn't need to worry.*

*Isn't Olive Witch Forest more wonderful now than ever? I
mean, now that Father's come and it's his place, too. Maybe it's
because I feel like I've always known him. Probably because I
can see I'm a lot like him, and especially like Anne. I think I*

got my dandelion hair from them both.

I love you, Hannah. It's not because I need you. In fact I love you even more, because I don't need you the same as I used to. When you and Father watched over me, I never felt alone. You listened to me and helped me stop seeing wasps hiding under my bed. I'm not afraid of the dark, because you were there when I needed you.

There are times I forget you're a tree, because you have such a big heart. You'll never be just a tree to me. You've been my haven, except right after the tornado and after I got Father arrested.

Sometimes I think I want to go into the Forest Service. At supper, that's what we talked about. I told them what I knew about Hallie Daggett, because I'd written a report about her being the first woman who was a lookout. All four of the grownups… well, I guess Marian is a grownup too, even though I think of her as my friend. Anyway, all five of them said if I wanted a career in the Forest Service, they would help me. I'm not really sure. I just want to try being a girl for a while and maybe do more things with friends.

They said, "Pick your battle." That was something to think about. I'm probably battling all I can as it is. Mostly my battle is with myself, and you've been helping me with that, Hannah, so I can have wings.

You know the time I went to the fair at Morgan's school, and they weren't going to teach me to change a tire? They said it was because I'm a girl, and you know what Morgan said? He told them, "She most certainly is not!"

I like being a girl, even though I sometimes like to learn things the same as boys do.

I don't feel like a tiny piece on a board game, any more. If I ever do, I'll remember I can fly off it and leave the little squares behind.

If I have a daughter someday, I hope she'll be braver than I am. Maybe she'll be an eagle.

Hannah swayed again, as if to assure Hetty that she would get better and better at flying. Hetty placed the palms of her hands hard against Hannah's firm trunk then with arms outstretched, she laid her cheek firmly against the bark, to feel Hannah pressing her cheek.

I call Melinda every day. She'll be all right. She's happy, even if she misses Morgan. She's sure Morgan must be a really good Bronze Giant. But she's doing okay at home, because she knows he's looking out for her, even though he's gone. I think the reason Morgan will be fine, is because he loves her back.

That's the big thing, isn't it, Hannah? It's loving people back.

Hannah seemed to sigh with satisfaction, and swayed again, as if to rejoice that Hetty had learned the secret of flying.

ABOUT THE AUTHOR

Martha Sears West grew up daydreaming and climbing trees in Bethesda, Maryland. Now the Mother of three and grand-mother of ten, West hopes everyone with children can see teenagers as the joy and inspiration she found hers to be.

The author, who received her B.A. degree in linguistics from the University of Maryland, claims to have merely pro-vided the hand that jotted down the story. She feels Hetty composed this book herself; however, there is no evidence Hetty ever existed.

Hetty is the first novel by Martha Sears West. She has also written and illustrated *Longer than Forevermore; Rhymes and Doodles from a Wind-up Toy;* and *Jake, Dad and the Worm.*

COLOPHON

The Bembo Typeface

Bembo is a classic typeface that displays the characteristics that identify Old Style, humanist designs. It was drawn by Aldus Manutius and first used in 1496 for a 60-page text about a journey to Mount Aetna by a young humanist poet, Pietro Bembo, later a cardinal and secretary to Pope Leo X.

More recently, Bembo is the typeface used for volumes in the Everyman's Library series. Monotype Bembo is generally regarded as one of the most handsome revivals of Manutius' 15th century roman type.

The font size of the italic sections in Hetty is 13; otherwise, font size 12 has been used in the body of the text.

CPSIA information can be obtained
at www.ICGtesting.com
Printed in the USA
FFOW04n1614200314
4350FF